Ten Out of Ten

Ten Out of Ten

Inspiring Inventions & Innovations

Padma Jyoti Dr. G. S. Ayyappan

Ten Out of Ten (10/10)
Padma Jyoti Dr. G. S. Ayyappan
First Published: August, 2024
Published by

INDIAN UNIVERSITIES PRESS
Imprint of Bharathi Puthakalayam
7, Elango Salai, Teynampet, Chennai - 600 018
044 -24332424, 24332924, 24330024
Email: bharathiputhakalam@gmail.com | www.thamizhbooks.com

Rs.100/-
Printed at Printech, Chennai - 600 005.

CONTENTS

The Missile man of India, Dr. A.B.J. Abdul Kalam's unparalleled dream that our country should shine as a nation of inventors. People's Scientist Padma Jyothi Dr. Ayyappan carries that ideal on his shoulders and is working for it. He travels all over Tamil Nadu and performs a series of motivational lectures for school children, college students, teachers, professors and science researchers. In the midst of heavy office and laboratory workload, the People's Scientist never forgets the ideals he received from Kalam.

He is a moral practitioner of Tamil. he

True Sadness Parar Hunger Observer

No one will do any evil

Lovely and disrespectful

Karma is the eye.

What's the point of that? His duty is to make this nation the land of success for inventors. Mahatma Gandhi often quoted the incomparable Upanishadic phrase Manasa, Vacha, Karmana. If what a person thinks in his mind, what he says and what he does – manasa, vacha, karma – is the same – then he is sure to achieve his goal. People Scientist is fulfilling his vision of becoming a nation of inventors with hundreds of new inventions in his mind, word and deed.

He was a brilliant inventor too. He holds of more than twenty patents in his name. But he is a mentor who guides the next generation of scientists to become innovators. Ten out of ten The Inspiring Inventions and Innovations is the seventh book that expands the motivation and purpose in that direction! I am born to achieve, I am born to win, I am born to rule - this book should be read and benefited by every student who grows up with the goal.

Among the inventions of the People's Scientist Dr. Ayyappan, one of my favorite invention is the tool to detect eight diseases. He describes it in detail in the fourth chapter of this book. His invention, the only tool to diagnose eight diseases, is used all over the world today. I have said many times that he should write a separate book on this. How an inventor evolves. What makes someone an inventor. Nikolai Tesla used to say that it would suddenly appear within me like a flash of lightning. This book brilliantly describes the secret and the stepsinvolvedthrough 10inventions and innovations.

During the Covidpandemic, there was a huge compulsion to vaccinate millions of people around the world. Not just in the metropolis... Humanity has to be saved by transporting vaccines (free of cost) to remote areas such as hamlets and tribal people. The temperature of the vaccine should be maintained at 18-20°C. They have to be refrigerated in boxes. Ice cubes don't endure. So the People's Scientist Dr G.S. Ayyappan invented an vaccine cooler. What a great achievement that the world used it. Isn't he a great man who saved humanity from disaster? He has been nominated for several international awards for the same. He will be honoured soon. The fifth chapter talks about this invention.

Today, all developed economies in the world are guided economies of innovators and innovators. The goal of the Indian motherland is to transform itself into a five trillion dollar economy. For that, we have to work hard with understanding in many ways. We are fortunate in the 21st century that India has 35 percent of its population (18 to 30 years old) in the world. So if we mould the youth into an army of unparalleled scientific inventions and innovations, we can conquer the world.

The Global Innovation Index has been published annually since 2007 by the World Intellectual Property Organization in collaboration with Cornell University. It is a sad reality that despite the remarkable achievements of our country in terms of industrial licenses, service sector licenses and technology based application licenses, only 5 out of 100 applicants got patended. But it is a record that our country has reached 46th position in the World Innovator Rankings in 2021 from 76th position in 2019.

If great scholars like our People Scientist Dr. G.S. Ayyappan guide the right way to the young minds, we can polish the great pearls of our soil and produce great inventors and improve the status of our country.

After Independence, Green Revolution, White Revolution, Blue Revolution (Massive Growth in Fisheries Production), Space Research Surge (ISRO), Nuclear Power Development (Bhabha Atomic Research Centre), the biotechnology revolution and the information technology revolution (satellite) subsequently achieved self-sufficiency in science. Behind each of these revolutions were great men and scientists. Dr. M.S. Swaminathan (Green Revolution), Dr. Kurien (White Revolution), Vikram Sarabhai (Space Exploration), Homi Jehangir Bhabha (Atomology), Dr. A.b.J Abdul Kalam can go on like this.

What India needs now is the Innovation Revolution and this Ten out of Ten tells us that it has just begun. The great man who will be known in history for this great revolution is the people's scientist Dr. G.S. Ayyappan! That hope will no doubt come to everyone who reads this book.

It is the duty of all of us to take this book to millions of youth of India – Entrepreneurship and Talent Pool. Let us stand shoulder to shoulder with the mission of the People's Scientist. Science will win.

Congratulations.

Ayesha Ira. Natarajan
Writer & Educator
Sahitya Academy Award Winner
Cuddalore

GREETING

According to Valluvan, "Those who know the virtue of the wise, know the friendship of the wise, know the skill", it is not surprising that everyone loves the friendship of the Chief Scientist Dr. G.S. Ayyappan. The number ten is the perfect number for those who are just starting out on their own, and for anyone who wants to call the next new chapter of their career. Yes! I am talking about his book "Ten out of Ten".

The line in Bharathi's new Aathichudi "Raise the stitch" is something that is deeply ingrained in me. For many, elevating women is just a matter of speaking on stage. One of the practical implementers is our chief scientist Ayyappan. He would invite his wife Sangeetha Ayyappan and his daughter Selvi Vaishnavi to participate in the reception and music programmes, art exhibitions and other functions he visited.

He has the generosity of getting people like me to participate in almost all kinds of events. From the description of the inventions of the students in this book, it is clear that he is a man who admires them.

Those who use the number "ten" are born to lead, either naturally or in some way. They are leaders and innovators. They are self-confident. They are good at doing it themselves. I think we can all agree that under their leadership and innovation skills he deserves a great validation. From the awards he has received, the great services he has performed, the positions and responsibilities he has held, it is clear that our Ayyappan took ten incarnations like Dasavataram.

Our Dr. Ayyappan uses all the opportunities for self-development which cannot be bought, no matter how much money he pays. It is an exaggeration to say that the person who used ten fingers on the computer keyboard and ten different brains with ten heads like Ravana.

The way our Dr. Ayyappan describes ten fascinating inventions and innovations in this book is wonderful! Sir C.V., who has made us all proud. He spoke about the Raman award, the "Fluropath", a tool used to diagnose eight diseases and the reasons for it.

He also encouraged his students by explaining some of their inventions. Dr. Ayyappan, the author of this book, has astonished us by describing the invention of Nigerian school girls. He talks about the inventions and creations of young scientists. He has entertained the readers with stories and illustrations to attract thoughts, better understanding and impression.

The author has explained the origin of the invention in many places in a way that the layman can understand. Those who read this book will know that he aims to spread science among the public, students and teachers in various 1 Places in Tamilnadu. You are a scientist who has won many ideas by his writing, deeds and speeches.

Ayyappan who does not hesitate to prevent or spoil! Even if you win, the leader will not be arrogant! You have risen to the top with tireless hard work and talent! I wish you many years of health, happiness, family, friends and friendship as you have the knowledge, ability and motivation to do many more things in the field of education, language and youth development.

It is my earnest request that your books continue to be published. I wish this book to be in everyone's hands.

This book is a must read for aspiring students and young scientists. It is my desire that this book should reach all schools.

The mother with love
P. Lakshmi Lakshmanan
Retired Government School Headmaster, Thiruporur, Chennai

Dear ones with a thoughtful heart! Friends who are always living with the hunger for knowledge! My dear and dignified students who are living with the ideal dream of "I am born to achieve, born to conquer, born to rule"! What's the next book? The wonderful Readers who are always eagerly waiting for the new ideas to be presented as book! I convey my heartfelt greetings to all of you through these words.

It is well known that being the precursor of research, invention or innovation, i.e., its source, the birthplace, and the homeland, are inspiration, curiosity, and creativity. The book, titled "Ten out of Ten", talks about the ten-best, the most inspiring, fascinating inventions and innovations that have appeared in the past and recent times. I'd like to discuss and share it with you. I am not going to say much about the in-depth knowledge or the techniques behind these inventions or innovations, but instead, I have described in greater detail the root cause of the invention and the way in which the invention originated.

In my second book, I have dealt with the significance of the mother tongue, the sweetness of the Tamil language, and the specialty of numbers. In the first chapter of this book, I am going to explain a special thing that connects numbers and the characteristics of people. In this chapter, I will also explain how best friends should be and how one should not be, which I have listened on a radio show. I've explained all in detail on the topic "Numbers and Friends".

In the second chapter, we will discuss in the title "Let us Learn Something". Let us start the chapter with the topic title "Discovery, Invention & Innovation". I'll introduce you to the discovery, fiction or invention, and innovation, as well as the connection and differences between them. In order to capture your thoughts, for a better understanding, and to inculcate in my mind. I am narrating it here and there with a few stories and illustrations.

In the third chapter, I have presented about the 1 out of 10, titled "Power that drives the Pacemaker", a wonderful invention that saves our lives. Princeton, a physicist from Singapore, who last his father in a critical medical problem, made a wonderful invention later in life with an inspiration. He said, "No one should die like my father anymore". A force driving the pacemaker is what I have explained in great detail, with pictures for easy understanding.

In the fourth chapter, one of my best inventions, which fetched me the highest civilian award, in the name of a Nobel laureate Sir C.V. Raman. I have explained about the "A tool that Diagnosis Eight Infectious Diseases", a global invention that won the Raman Award. The innovation is named as "Fluropath". I have described the phenomenon that led to the innovation and the manner in which it was made. I belief that, very few inventions or innovations are made in laboratories, and most of them have occurred when we look closely at the problems and nature that are happening around us. In that sense, at the lowest cost, in the simplest possible way, if my innovation is a global achievement, then why would I call this simply as Innovation? It would not be an exaggeration to say that has earned me the name of "People's Scientist" among the people, it's my "A Compact Tool that diagnoses Eight diseases".

In the fifth chapter, another of my research findings is "A tool that prescribes the Medicines or drugs by itself". The name we have given to this innovation is "Anti-Biogram" or "Multi-Drug Resistance System (MDR)". This invention is a continuation of diagnostic tool that we came across in the preceding chapter, about which I have given the explanations with detailed pictures.

In the sixth chapter, I have explained the invention of a life-saving tool, the "Vaccine Cooler". This is also one of my research findings. In this section, I have explained the problems and side effects of conventional vaccine coolers that have been in use for many decades, and I have explained about the device, which is being developed at a very low cost, preventing wastage of medicines, and which will soon come out as a lifesaving noble tool.

In the seventh chapter, the mind blowing fifth invention, which we are about to know is an invention that amazes the whole world. Yes. "Water-powered Motor Vehicle". What? Bikes run on Water? Wonder! Well yes. A Brazilian inventor has developed a water-powered motorcycle. I have explained about this invention in this chapter.

In the eighth chapter, I have explained the "Self-Driving Wheelchair" which is an invention that has been developed exclusively for people suffering from paralysis or rheumatoid arthritis. I have described an event that was the root cause of the innovation, the manner in which the innovation came into being, and the innovator, and I am feeling very proud to say that the innovator of the innovation is one of my students.

In the ninth chapter, I have described the seventh inspiring innovation, "Anti-Puncturing Vahana Chakras". Under no circumstances will the tyres of the vehicle be punctured, even if the nail pierces it, the tyre will not explode, the vehicle will not derail and roll on the road, accidents will not occur, and there will be no loss of life at all. If so, do you also think it is a classic invention! Yes. I have shared the details of this in great detail in this chapter.

In chapter 10, I have described the invention of four Nigerian school-girls in Africa, which is entitled "The Urine-Powered Generator". The four teenage girls have developed a power generator that can be operated with just 1 liter of urine, thereby keeping the 100W bulb glowing for up to six hours. I have explained the details of it very clearly in this chapter.

Ninth out Ten (9 of 10), the "Life-Saving Fan Rod" is another mind-blowing invention that we are going to learn in chapter 11. I have been inspired by the word of Dr. APJ Kalam, "Rather becoming a successful Scientist, we have the responsibility to create young and budding Scientists". The seed of science is sown, the invention of an achievement, an innovation of a life-saving noble instrument was developed. This innovator of this innovation has won India's "Young Scientist" award. When I say that my student created a noble instrument of lifesaving, it makes my mind happy, feeling proud, an invention that ensures that behind every invention there is an impulse, i.e., inspiration. In this chapter, I have explained in detail some of the incident that took place in his life, the background of the innovation, and the innovation.

In the twelfth chapter, Tenth out of Ten (10 of 10), another fascinating innovation that we are going to see is the "Anti-Skidding Two-wheeler". The innovator is another student of mine. While driving a two-wheeler, when turning to one side, is sure to skit if the angle between the road and the vehicle falls below a certain degree, and at that time the third wheel comes out automatically on the side to which the vehicle is tilted and starts running like a three-wheeler. Hence, the bike will not skid. In this section, I have explained in great detail the manner in which this innovation was made and its implementation.

Have you read my previous two books that came out as a publication of the Bharathi Puththakalayam, titled "Pancha Dhandras – Want to Be a Scientist?" and "This is how I Conquered – The Secret of Success (SoS)". I hope that you might have read and enjoyed it. When I was writing these books, I wanted this book to reach all over the state of Tamil Nadu. But this publisher has made these books available in the hands of the Tamil speaking people living in every corner of the world. It has been well received from Germany, Qatar, Saudi Arabia, Sri Lanka and all over the country. When the readers contacted me and talked to me, I felt very happy. Now both the books are available on Amazon as well.

My dear friends, who consider reading books to be a breath! My dear and respected students who says, "It is my dream to achieve by reading"! The perfect treat for your hunger for reading is waiting for you to "Ten Out of Ten". Shall we go in? Are you ready?

Ever Yours
Dr. G.S. Ayyappan

"One best book is equal to hundred good friends but one Best friend is equal to a library - Dr A.P.J.Abdul kalam

Dear readers, in the first chapter of my second book, "Ippadithan Jeyithen - The Secret of Success (SoS)", I had explained the importance of mother tongue, the sweetness of Tamil language and the importance of numbers. In the first chapter of this book, I will discuss a special link between numbers and the characteristics of people. In this chapter, I will explain these concepts that I heard on a radio program (FM) about how best friends should be and how bad friendships should be.

When we study numbers in English, they say that the number 13 is not good at all. The number 13 is an example of infidelity. When the city of Chandigarh was formed, it was divided into sectors. At that time, 13-number sector was planned, but the 13-sector was built as graveyard called the cremation ground. It may even be foolishness. But even today there is no sector number 13 in Chandigarh.

But all the numbers in Tamil have a speciality. Especially the number three, five, nine, twelve, eighteen, twenty-seven, forty-one, each number has a special significance. For example, I explained the significance of three and five in the last book. The planets are nine (Navagrahas), the zodiac signs are twelve, the Puranas are eighteen; Eighteen Vedic Epics; The protective hands of Durga are eighteen; There are eighteen steps of Lord Ayyappa at holy Sabarimala. The stars are twenty-seven. A mandalam is forty-one. A lot can be said about the excellence of numbers like this.

I am going to share here about a few new concepts that I heard on a radio program on the topic of "Numbers and Friends". That is, when talking about good friends and bad friends, that is, good friendship and bad friendship, they compared it to some numbers. I was really surprised. Here's the thing!

Good friends should always be like the number 9-nine. That is, if nine is added to another nine, eighteen is obtained (9 + 9 = 18). If you add two digits of the result, you get only nine (1 + 8 = 9). Similarly, if three nines are added, the sum comes as twenty-seven (9 + 9 + 9 = 27). 2 + 7 = 9. No matter how many times you add it up, the sum comes to nine.

$$9 + 9 = 18; 1 + 8 = 9$$

$$9 + 9 + 9 = 27; 2 + 7 = 9$$

$$9 + 9 + 9 + 9 = 36; 3 + 6 = 9$$

$$9 + 9 + 9 + 9 + 9 = 45; 4 + 5 = 9$$

$$9 + 9 + 9 + 9 + 9 + 9 = 54; 5 + 4 = 9$$

$$9 + 9 + 9 + 9 + 9 + 9 + 9 = 63; 6 + 3 = 9$$

$$9 + 9 + 9 + 9 + 9 + 9 + 9 + 9 = 72; 7 + 2 = 9$$

$$9 + 9 + 9 + 9 + 9 + 9 + 9 + 9 + 9 = 81; 8 + 1 = 9$$

$$9 + 9 + 9 + 9 + 9 + 9 + 9 + 9 + 9 + 9 = 90; 9 + 0 = 9$$

$$9 + 9 + 9 + 9 + 9 + 9 + 9 + 9 + 9 + 9 + 9 = 99; 9 + 9 = 18 = 1 + 8 = 9$$

$$9 + 9 + 9 + 9 + 9 + 9 + 9 + 9 + 9 + 9 + 9 + 9 = 108; 1 + 0 + 8 = 9$$

......

$$20 * 9 = 180 = 1 + 8 + 0 = 9$$

......

Friends should be like number 9. That is, no matter how many good friends you have, that good friendship will never change; Its character never changes. It is also clear that they will still be good friends. It is also the account of life.

If the number 9 is a good friend, then if you join with any friends of inferior quality, then even a good friend will be reduced. For example, when any number other than zero is added to nine, its sum is the same number with which we add nine. For example, if the number 9 is added to the number 6 (9 + 6 = 15; 1 + 5 = 6), its digit sum becomes 6. For example

$$9 + 1 = 10; 1 + 0 = 1$$

$$9 + 2 = 11; 1 + 1 = 2$$

$$9 + 3 = 12; 1 + 2 = 3$$

$$9 + 4 = 13; 1 + 3 = 4$$

$$9 + 5 = 14; 1 + 4 = 5$$

$$9 + 6 = 15; 1 + 5 = 6$$

$$9 + 7 = 16; 1 + 6 = 7$$

$$9 + 8 = 17; 1 + 7 = 8$$

That is, if a good friend joins a friend with bad adventure, that good friend will also be ruined. The number 8 is an example of bad friendship. That is, the lowest friendship is compared to 8. That is, our numerology says that when friends of any rank, except number one, join with inferior friends, he goes down one level further from his level. For example

$$8 + 2 = 10; 1 + 0 = 1$$

$$8 + 3 = 11; 1 + 1 = 2$$

$$8 + 4 = 12; 1 + 2 = 3$$

$$8 + 5 = 13; 1 + 3 = 4$$

$$8 + 6 = 14; 1 + 4 = 5$$

$$8 + 7 = 15; 1 + 5 = 6$$

$$8 + 8 = 16; 1 + 6 = 7$$

$$8 + 9 = 17; 1 + 7 = 8$$

❑

"In the present-day world when the corpus of known knowledge is multidisciplinary and products and services are complex, it is often not possible to have a loner as an innovator. Most of the discoveries and innovation are team efforts." - A.P.J. Abdul Kalam

In this chapter, we will try to find out what the true meaning of discovery, innovation, and invention is, and how these three are driven by research. The role and responsibilities of the discoverer, inventor, and innovator will also be well explained. After reading this chapter, we will also learn about the qualifications required to become a discoverer, inventor, or innovator. First revelation, let me describe a little bit about discovery, invention and innovation.

Discovery (Revelation):

- Revelation or discovery is the expression of something that already exists, but which people do not know.

- Discovery refers to discovering or revealing the reality.

- Something exists naturally, but it is not known to ordinary people. Discovery means finding it and revealing it to the world.

- For example, Sir Isaac Newton revealed or discovered force of gravity, called gravitational force, which is a matter inherent in nature.

- No one knows why any objects are attracted towards the center of the Earth until Sir Isaac Newton, whom we are so familiar with, discovers the force of gravity.

In a Tamil film, a comedian robs the temple money from the temple hundi and then draws a small circle as if asking for forgiveness of sins and says to God, "Hello God. I'm very good, and I'll give you a share of the money I've got, and now I'm going to throw all the money upwards, and whatever falls into that circle is for you, only whatever money is left out of the circle is for me". Then, he will throw the money upwards with maximum force, so that very little money falls into that circle. "Oh my God. You are great, you are not greedy. Thank you, God," he would say, adding, "This is your share" and throwing only one or two of the coins that had fallen for the little vat, and putting it in a nearby hundi. The hero will immediately say that, "Oh my dear friend! You're too bad. I don't want to confine God into a small circle. I will point to the vast sky and say, "O God! You are a very kind-hearted man. Now I will throw all the money upwards. God! Take as much money as you want and give it to me if you have anything left. I'll only take what you give me". He began to throw all the money upwards. " Oh, My God, you are so kind, perhaps God felt this is enough. That is why he returned all the money to me. He would deceive God by saying, "God is Great". This is a comedy scene from the movie.

Similarly, in the name of offering to God, if the offering is thrown upwards in the sky, people are superstitious to believe that God will accept it and give us the rest to use. This is all stories. Let us come to reality.

Newton doesn't like school at all. Every day, he would pack his lunch and go to a nearby apple orchard with a rope-cot, lie down under an apple tree, sleep well, and sometimes start counting the apples and spend his time. "Why do all the apples fall from the tree to the bottom? Why didn't you go up? " he asked himself a question. By his intense efforts, after few studies, he declared that the reason why all objects come down from the sky is because any object is attracted towards the center of the earth and that force is the force of gravity. Although there were a lot of contradictions at first, later on, this concept was accepted and it is well-known that Newton did extensive research on gravity and brought many discoveries, inventions and innovations.

Insulin was released at the University of Toronto in 1921 by Sir Frederick G. Ponting, Charles H. Best, and JJR MacLeod, and later it was further refined and published by James B. Collip.

Christopher Columbus! Or Kennithe line! There is still controversy going on. "Who invented America? If you ask a question, we will all say, "Columbus was the inventor of America."But that was the wrong answer. Why the question itself is wrong? No one has invented or created America. There was already a continent in the world called America, but the common people did not know until he revealed that message, so from now on the question has to be asked correctly first. "Who revealed or discovered America?". Well yes. Columbus revealed America. The word invention should not be used here, it must be said that it was Columbus who revealed or discovered America. My dear friends! Do you understand and I think you will agree with me?

You must have watched discovery channel, which discovers, explores and presents many things that we don't know about.

As a revealing or discovery Scientist:

One who exposes unknown things to people or to this world is called a "discoverer" or a "revealing scientist". Discoverer should be prepared to travel a lot, to do adventures, to face any kind of hardships, trials, and problems, and to be ready to eat whatever is available. Only they can become great, accomplished scientists.

Invention:

Let us now explore in detail about invention

➢ Invention refers to creat something that does not already exist. It is also known as fiction.

➢ Invention refers to an individual's ideas (idea) or new ideas, theory, or products derived from scientific research.

➢ Invention can be a theory, law, definition, new ideas, mathematical formulas, process, or materials.

➢ The role of invention helps the world, to people, to benefit people with something unique, something that was not there before.

For example, Alexander Graham Bell, the inventor of the Telephone is an invention. Until his invention occurred., no one could not communicate and talk to anyone who was far away. In the early days, people would stand on top of a tree or a mountain and speak in a loud voice. The first man to communicate with a metal wire was none other than Graham Bell, and that was the invention.

The first microscope was invented by Zacharias Janssen. In the name of micro+ scope, a purpose or tool to visualize anything in the size of a few microns (10^{-6} m). It is a laboratory tool used to study objects that are too small for the naked eye to see. A microscope is a scientific tool used to study small objects and structures using a microscope. So far, a number of types of microscopic tools have been invented; some of which are: optical microscope, electron microscope, tunneling microscope, atomic microscope, and so on.

Charles Babbage invented the computer. Electricity was invented by Benjamin Franklin and the thermometer was invented by Gabriel Fahrenheit. The table below shows the best outcomes, findings, the name of the inventor and the year of Invention.

Invention	Inventor	year
Electricity	Benjamin Franklin	1759
Centigrade scale	Anders Celsius	-
Radio	Guglielmo Marconi	1895
Thermometer	Gabriel Fahrenheit	1714
Electric Bulb	Thomas Edison	1879
Telescope	Hans Lippershey and Zacharias Janssen; Then Galileo	1608
Air Brake	Westinghouse	1869
Amplitude modulation	Reginald Fesston	-
Anemometer (wind speed)	Leon Batista Alberti	1450
Barometer	Evangelista Doricelli	-
Cathode Ray Tube	Ferdinand Brown	1897
Telegram	Samuel Morse	1830
Automobile	Carl Benz	1885
Transformer	Michael Faraday	1885
Electromagnetic induction	Michael Faraday	1830
Quantum Mechanics	Werner Heisenberg, Max Bourne and Pasquel Jordan	1924
Nuclear reactor	Enrico Fermi	1942
Plane	Wright Brothers	1903
Camera	Nisefor Nibs	1816
L. ED (LED)	Oleg Lochev, Nick Holonyac	1962
Force of gravity	Sir Isaac Newton	1687

Battery	Alessandro Volta	1799
Induction motor	Nikola Tesla	1885
Diesel Engine	Rudolf Diesel	1858
Dynamite	Alfred Nobel	1867
Elevator	Elisha Otis	1853
Mobile Phone	Martin Cooper	1973
Printing Press	Johannes Gutenberg	1440
Steam engine	Thomas Newcoman	1698
Railway Engine	George Stephenson	-
Telephone	Alexander Graham Bell	1876
Seismograph	John Milne	1839
Electric Generator	Michael Faraday	1831
Television	John Logie Bird	1927
Calculator	Blaze Pascal	1642
Refrigerator	William Cullen	1927
Atomic bomb		
	Robert Oppenheimer, Edward Teller and others	1945
Air Conditioner	Willis Carrier	1902
Radar	Sir Robert Alexander Watson-Watt	1939
Transistor	John Bardeen, Walter Brattain and William Shockley	1947
Galvanometer	JohanN Sweeger	1820
Laser	Theodore H. Maiman	1969
Rocket Engine	Robert Goddard	
Typewriter	Christopher Latham Scholz	1878
Polythene	Eric Fawcett	1933
Osmosis	Jean Antoine Nolet	1748
Electrons	JJ Thomson	1897

Protons	Ernest Rutherford	1911
Inert gases	Sir William Ramsay	1894
Radioactivity	Henry Beckerell	1896
Schedule	Dmitry Mendeleev	1869
Oxygen	Carl Wilhelm	1773
Hydrogen	Henry Cavendish	1766
Atoms	John Dalton	1803
Acid (LSD)	Albert Hoffman	1938
Ionic bonds	Swande August Arrhenius	1884
Aluminium	Charles Martin Hall	1886
PH Meter	Arnold O. Beckman	1934
Synthetic Rubber	Fritz Hoffman	1909
Titanium	William Kroll (cricketer)	1940
Radium	Mary Slodo	1898
Penicillin	Alexander Fleming	1928
Doxol	Monroe Wall and Mansukh Wani	-
Anesthesia	William Morton (cricketer)	-
Pasteurization	Louis Pasteur	-
LCD (LCD)	George H. Helmier	1888
Aspirin	Felix Hoffman	1899
D. My. A (DNA)	Sequencer Lloyd M. Smith	1987
Blood group	Carl Landsteiner	1900
Calcium	Humphrey Davy	1808
Cholera vaccine	Waldemar Hoffkin	1892
Rubella vaccine	Maurice Hillman	1963
Polio vaccine	Jonas Edward Stock	-
Anthrax vaccine	Louis Pasteur	-
X-ray	William Roentgen (cricketer)	1895

Vitamin	Qasimir Funk	1912
Homeopathy and Allopathy	Samuel Hahnemann	-
Go	Robert Hooke	1665
Nucleus	Robert Brown	-

Source: *www.ownguru.com*

To become an inventor:

Invention generally takes a few years to several years. Sometimes, one's invention is recognized even after one's death, and therefore the three P's needed to become a successful, inventor is the Passion, Patience, Persistence or Perseverance. This may also require creative thinking, untiring efforts, team or collaborative efforts.

Innovation:

Many people are confused between invention and innovation, and some say that the two are the same, but in my opinion, they are completely different.

- Invention refers to an individual's ideas or new ideas or products derived from scientific research.

- Whereas innovation is giving a new shape to inventions or creating a new kind of use.

- Sometimes, innovation is referred as refining or improving upon the previous invention.

- It can even be said that innovating is the commercialization of invention.

For example, the phone is an invention; A mobile phone is an innovative creation. The computer is an invention; A laptop is an innovation, i.e. improved invention, and there are many such innovative creations; However, many laws, definitions, and principles have not yet been applied or found an application.

For example, Seebeck's effect; "When two metal wires are joined together to form two junction terminals named A&B and when one junction (say A) is kept on cold ice and the other junction (say B) is placed in hot water, then a voltage (emf-Electro-Motive Force) is produced between the two wires. This emf is called as thermo-emf. This is an invention. The application of Seebeck's effect is thermocouples; which is used as Sensor or transducer to measure the unknown temperature.

Later, a physics student named Peltier replaced the battery instead of connecting to the Galvanometer (Ammeter) across the wires by mistake. Due to this, the junction of the hot water has cooled down and turned into ice; and the other junction kept in the ice cubes began to melt. This is an innovation. It was later announced in 1868 as the "Peltier effect". But there has been no suitable application since the innovation of the Peltier effect, till last decads.

Due to the drastic advancement in the invention of semiconductor physics, with technological advances, were invented in the late 1970s as the Peltier blocks (Thermo-Electric Module-TEM) as a cooling device. TEM is an innovation and the Peltier effect are the innovative creation.

Those who are enthusiastic, think positively and creatively, who can create something unique, can all become the innovators. Innovation can happen even in a day. Sometimes it can take a week, month or even years. It is very easy to become an innovator. That's why students can quickly and gracefully become innovators. To become an innovator, the only thing needed is creativity.

Research:

The meaning of research can be realized by splitting the word research into Re + Search. When you're constantly searching for something, that leads to research. The researcher is called a "Scientist". A Scientist can do research to reveal or discover invent or innovate something. A Scientist's role is to explore what's going on around them. I have also explained more elaborately about research, types of research and how to conduct research, which are referred from the website *(Source:https://www.questionpro.com/blog/what-is-research/).*

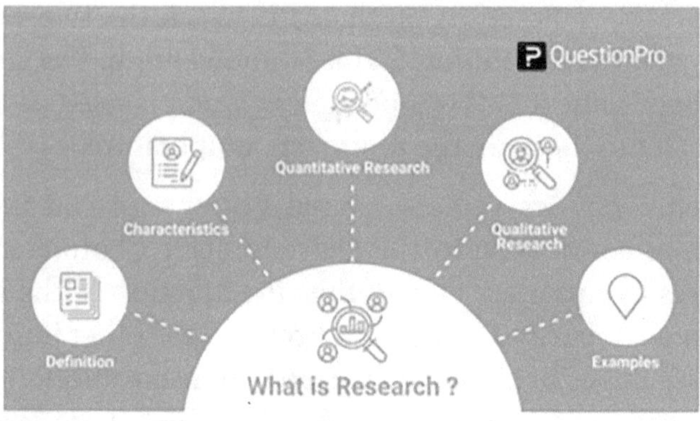

What is Research?

Research is the careful consideration of study regarding a particular concern or research problem using scientific methods. According to the American sociologist Earl Robert Babbie, "research is a systematic inquiry to describe, explain, predict, and control the observed phenomenon. It involves inductive and deductive methods. "Inductive methods analyze an observed event, while deductive methods verify the observed event. Inductive approaches are associated with qualitative research, and deductive methods are more commonly associated with quantitative analysis.

What are the characteristics of research?

- Good research follows a systematic approach to capture accurate data. Researchers need to practice ethics and a code of conduct while making observations or drawing conclusions.

- The analysis is based on logical reasoning and involves both inductive and deductive methods.

- Real-time data and knowledge are derived from actual observations in natural settings.

- There is an in-depth analysis of all data collected so that there are no anomalies associated with it.

- It creates a path for generating new questions. Existing data helps create more research opportunities.

- It is analytical and uses all the available data so that there is no ambiguity in inference.

- Accuracy is one of the most critical aspects of research. The information must be accurate and correct. For example, laboratories provide a controlled environment to collect data. Accuracy is measured in the instruments used, the calibrations of instruments or tools, and the experiment's final result.

What are main purposes of Research?

♣ **Exploratory:** As the name suggests, researchers conduct exploratory studies to explore a group of questions. The answers and analytics may not offer a conclusion to the perceived problem. It is undertaken to handle new problem areas that haven't been explored before. This exploratory data analysis process lays the foundation for more conclusive data collection and analysis.

♣ **Descriptive:** It focuses on expanding knowledge on current issues through a process of data collection. Descriptive research describe the behavior of a sample population. Only one variable is required to conduct the study. The three primary purposes of descriptive studies are describing, explaining, and validating the findings. For example, a study conducted to know if top-level management leaders in the 21st century possess the moral right to receive a considerable sum of money from the company profit.

♣ **Explanatory:** Causal research or explanatory research is conducted to understand the impact of specific changes in existing standard procedures. Running experiments is the most popular form. For example, a study that is conducted to understand the effect of rebranding on customer loyalty.

Comparative analysis chart for a better understanding:

	Exploratory Research	Descriptive Research	Explanatory Research
Approach used	Unstructured	Structured	Highly structured
Conducted through	Asking questions	Asking questions	By using hypotheses.
Time	Early stages of decision making	Later stages of decision making	Later stages of decision making

It begins by asking the right questions and choosing an appropriate method to investigate the problem. After collecting answers to your questions, you can analyze the findings or observations to draw reasonable conclusions.

When it comes to customers and market studies, the more thorough your questions, the better the analysis. You get essential insights into brand perception and product needs by thoroughly collecting customer data through surveys and questionnaires. You can use this data to make smart decisions about your marketing strategies to position your business effectively.

To make sense of your study and get insights faster, it helps to use a research repository as a single source of truth in your organization and manage your research data in one centralized data repository.

Types of research methods and Examples

Research methods are broadly classified as Qualitative and Quantitative. Both methods have distinctive properties and data collection methods.

Qualitative methods: Qualitative research is a method that collects data using conversational methods, usually open-ended questions. The responses collected are essentially non-numerical. This method helps a researcher understand what participants think and why they think in a particular way.

Types of qualitative methods include:

- One-to-one Interview

- Focus Groups

- Ethnographic studies

- Text Analysis

- Case Study

Quantitative methods: Quantitative methods deal with numbers and measurable forms. It uses a systematic way of investigating events or data. It answers questions to justify relationships with measurable variables to either explain, predict, or control a phenomenon.

Types of quantitative methods include:

- ♣ Survey research

- ♣ Descriptive research

- ♣ Correlational research

Remember, it is only valuable and useful when it is valid, accurate, and reliable. Incorrect results can lead to mistake and a leads to failure. It is essential to ensure that your data is:

- Valid – founded, logical, rigorous, and impartial.

- Accurate – free of errors and including required details.

- Reliable – other people who investigate in the same way can produce similar results.

- Timely – current and collected within an appropriate time frame.

- Complete – includes all the data you need to support your business decisions.

❑

A DEVICE TO POWER-UP THE PACEMAKER

"We cannot solve a problem by using the same kind of thinking we used when we created them." - Albert Einstein

The first mind-blowing Invention:

The first mind-blowing invention which we are going to explore is a Device to Power-up the Pacemaker. A device or a system, that always keeps the heart to beat smoothly with the "Nano Piezo Pacemaker". First of all, let's learn about the "Pace Maker" tool, its functions and its drawbacks. Are you ready? YES.

Pace Maker - an artificial valve

An important part of our body is the "heart". If the heartbeat stops, everything stops. At first, the blood flow stops. The blood will freeze. The flow of oxygen in the body will stop. Along with that, life will be subdued. There are two blood vessels i.e. valves that are very important for the processing of the "lub-dub" which keep the functioning of the heart steady.

It is called as "ventriculate" valve. These valves allow the blood to flow inside the heart at the time of saying "lub", and oxygen when it says "dub" without mixing it. When there are blockages in those blood vessels, if the valve is not functioning properly, there may be a heart attack i.e. chest pain or cardiac arrest, i.e., a stop to the heartbeat and even the risk of losing life.

If there is a blockage in these blood vessels, or if it is completely damaged, open heart or bypass surgery is performed. It is a major operation, in which they bypass the damaged valves and replaced it with a device called a "Pace Maker". During surgery, the heart is artificially pulsed with a device called a ventilator. After the operation is completed, the ventilator is removed first.

Just like that, the heart stops for a while. The electrical pulse will make the heart run again. If the heart beat resumes, it can be a successful operation. Or, the doctors would knead their hands and say the single word "SORRY" and leave.

The Pace Maker is an artificial tool that provides "lub-dub" and performs the job continuously and keeps the heart running smoothly. This pace maker tool is made up of crystals. What we are going to see is not about this "Pace Maker" tool.

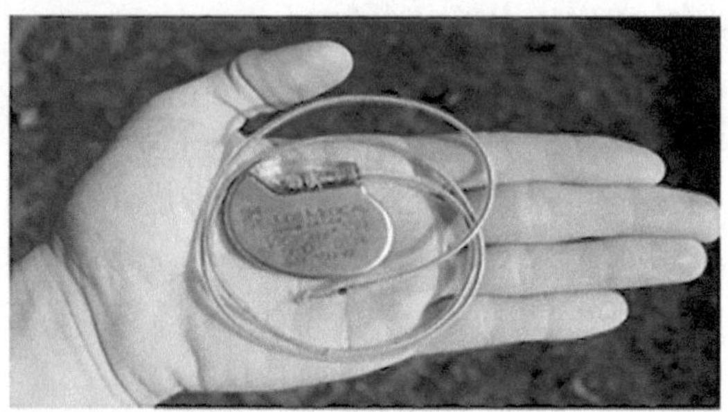

Root Cause of this Invention:

Let us first find out the root cause of this invention. There was a young man named Princeton in Singapore. He was studying in class XII. Suddenly Princeton's father suffered from heart attack and was admitted to a premier hospital there. All the necessary tests were carried out. After three days, it was decided that cardiac surgery would be performed. Princeton stayed with his father at the hospital and looked after him. The day of the operation came. Everything was ready; Surgeon and physicians including Anesthesiologist.

A hospital official called Princeton and asked him to read the conditions on the document "Declaration Form" on the permit and put a signature on it. Normally, wherever we are asked to sign, we will sign in a hurry, without even seeing what is written on the paper or the deed. If someone ask, "Why?". We'll say there's no time for that. But Princeton studied each of those conditions soberly.

The first condition is "The Success Rate after Surgery is 50-50% only. We cannot claim 100% Success"; "The percentage of success after surgery is only 50 per cent. If a patient dies, neither the doctors nor the hospital will be responsible for it." Yes. You have to accept it. Doctors are human beings too! They are not God! Princeton also agreed to the first condition.

The second condition. That's what made Princeton to think. "The estimated life time of the patient after surgery is around 8 to 9 years"; That means after the surgery, the patient's life expectancy is only 8-9 years." We are spending so much of money, time and perform the surgery. But Princeton could not accept that the life of the survivor was guaranteed only 8-9 years. He immediately asked the officer there for an explanation. The officer replied, I don't know all that. If you put your signature only in the places I mentioned, they will immediately take your father inside the operation theatre. But Princeton did not agree. The officer said, Go and talk to the PRO. That PRO also replied that "I don't know. Why don't you go and talk to the Doctor?". Prince to didn't give up either. He went there and looked at the doctor and said, "Sir, I don't understand this second condition."

The doctor patiently summoned Princeton and made him sit down next to him, and explained the doubt he had asked. It was that explanation that made Princeton to think. Later, with Princeton's extreme efforts and brilliant research, a solution to the problem could be found. I also understand and I am able to read your mind-voice. "What's that problem?" Let me share with you the doctor's explanation.

"Do you know what's the problem with your dad?" asked Doctor. Princeton asserted, "My dad was told that he had a heart problem and that there were three places blockage in the heart vessels (valves). To treat this problem, a heart bypass surgery is mandate and a 'Pace Maker' is to be fitted". The doctor replied, "You are right. Now I'll also tell you about the problem in that PaceMaker machine. Listen carefully."

"This pace maker tool is made up of crystals something like a quartz material. It's an artificial valve. There is nothing wrong in its functioning. It is equipped with a battery to make it function properly. It's a lithium battery called button cell. The life span of this battery is just ten years from the date of manufacturing. That means, it will only work for ten years from the day the battery is manufactured. It will take a year or two when a battery is made, goes somewhere and is available to the consumer like the operating theater in the hospital. Therefore, when the battery is fitted into a Pace Maker device that puts it inside our body, its life span will be reduced to 8-9 years. That's why we say that the

life expectancy of those who fitted the Pace Maker is 8-9 years," explained the doctor very clearly. Princeton understood what its real problem was.

This event itself became an inspiration for Princeton. We know that for every invention or innovation, inspiration is the seed. It affected the mind of Princeton very deeply. "I think, I will find a wonderful solution later on", Princeton said, inscribing in his subconscious mind.

The operation also ended successful. His father also returned home in good health. But the Yama did not spare him. Within the next two years, he died with a different disease. A struggle in mind for Princeton, who lost his father. This problem should not happen to any other father or for the sack of any human-being again, as happened to his father and lost his father. He began to think seriously to give a solution. That was the inspiration and reason for his invention. The invention was later awarded with the "Nobel Prize", the world's greatest and prestigious award.

How the Invention was evolved?

Princeton was then in his third year of bachelor's degree in physics. His entire interest was all about finding a good solution to the Pace Maker problem somehow. He continued his efforts as a series of efforts, without any let-up. Throughout his gravity, Princeton was studying about the Piezo Electric effects thoroughly. You might wonder what is this "Piezo Electric"? No wonder, very soon you are going to become a Scientist – budding Scientist. Yes. You are started asking question.

Piezo Electric Device! Yes. Every day we use it on your mobile phone. The speaker used on your mobile phone is nothing but a Piezoelectric device and works on the principle of the Piezo Electric effect. Piezo Buzzers, we use regularly in our car

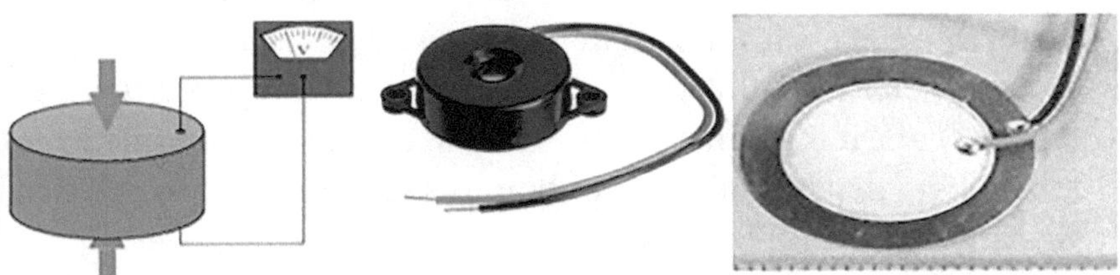

reversing, UPS, mini-projects and everything else You may have seen buzzers, in many electric or electronic appliances.

Piezo Electric Effect :

Piezo is an extension of PZT, which means a mixture of three materials called P-Platinum, Z-Zirconium, and T-Titanium. A mixture of these three materials constitutes a unique metal. This piezo mixture can be made like a coin as shown in figure above. Feel like there are two sides to a coin.

Piezo Electric Effect: *"When a mechanical force is applied between the opposite faces of PZT crystal, then e.m.f. will be produced across the faces of the crystal. Vice-versa; when an* *electrical potential is applied between the opposite faces of the crystal, mechanical vibration is produced across the face. Either it contracts or elongates."*

This PZT electrical effect is used in many applications. There are many applications such as a speaker on the mobile phone, a sound-making device called a buzzer, etc. Our Princeton was well versed in it all. He knew its essence very well. Later, what he chose for his Ph.D. thesis was also the piezo electric effect. That was the basis of his wonderful invention.

Research Work:

Princeton intensified his research work. No one can deny the evolving nano technology, its contribution, and applications. Millimeter is one thousand times the size of a meter. A micrometer is one-thousandth of a millimeter. The scale of the meter is 10^{-6}, i.e., the size of our hair is the size of a micrometer.

By the name implies "Nano car", I was really shocked and thrilled to see such a car. Whether the size of car is in the order of nanometer (10^{-9m}). No. It was just a name. Compared to other types of cars, it is smaller in size and less expensive. But this nano technology that we are talking about is something very small that we cannot see with our eyes.

To understand in a better way about the Nano technology and Nano world. Let us take a small fruit graps, whose size is in the order of few millimeter. Magnify or zoom up the size of graph to the level of 10^9. Then it is equivalent to the size of a globe or earth. Similarly, if we zoom down or using microscope to the level of 10^9; then you will find a different world. It is called as Nano world. The technology related to nano is called as Nano technology and has many unique features and applications such as Carbon nanotubes. It has been invented and used in the medical field and in micro-technologies.

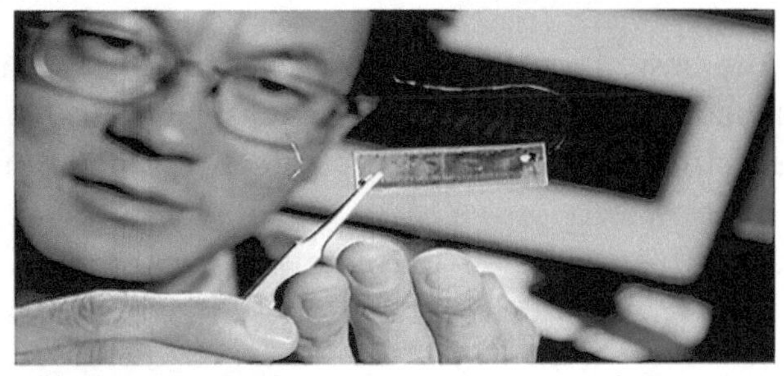

Nano Piezo Pace Maker:

Our Princeton, who was well versed in nano technology, designed a Nano-sized coil in the shape of the hair or fur in the eyeball, as shown in the picture. It is made up of an inorganic metal called the PZT. He connects it with the help of two nerves.

He then cuts off the blood vessels that pass through our heart and attaches this Nano-piezo coil to it. Now, the blood that passes through the blood vessels, also flows through the Nano-piezo coil.

The blood that first goes inward, then goes backwards. Due to the blood pressure in our body, both sides of the Nano-piezo contract and then expand. Because of this, voltage is generated in the Nano-piezo coil. With the help of the voltage now produced, is sufficient to power-up the PaceMaker fitted to the heart.

Now look at the miracle that is happening. As long as the heart beats, the flow of blood will continue. As long as there is blood flow, the Nano-piezo will continue to produce electricity. As long as there is power, the PaceMaker will keep running. As long as the Pace Maker runs, the heart will keep beating. Man's life is alive as long as the heart beats. This process will keep repeating like a cycle for infinite amount of time.

Therefore, the life of human may be prolonged. When the Pace Maker runs on a lithium battery, its life span is restricted to 8-9 years. But with the help of the Pace Maker through the Nano piezo coil, its lifetime is extended to be infinite.

Once the basic functionality was verified, it was extensively tested in many laboratories. After extensive clinical trials and intensive testing, the same was implanted into the human body and the Nano-piezo powered Pace Maker is now working successfully. This invention was admired by the whole world. Princeton was awarded with the Nobel Prize for his invention later.

My dear budding Scientists! Princeton's dream also became a reality, in line with the song that if you have a dream and keep trying it every day, it will come true one day. Yes. It became true. Every day we are witnessing many inventions such as angioplasty and angio-surgery to treat the heart related problems growing.

So, Friends! This invention is not a simple invention; not only in my opinion. For you too. It is a mind-blowing invention; Inspiring Invention! Yes or No? I hope you will agree with me. Okay. Next, shall we see what is the next inspiring invention or innovation in ten out of ten?

❑

A TOOL THAT DIAGNOSIS EIGHT INFECTIOUS DISEASES

"Innovation distinguishes between a leader and a follower." - Steve Jobs

The second mind-blowing Invention:

In this chapter, I will explain about one of my best innovation named as "A Tool That Diagnosis Eight Infectious Diseases", which fetched me the highest civilian award, in the name of a Nobel laureate Sir C.V. Raman. The innovation is named as "Fluropath".

I have described the phenomenon that led to the innovation and the manner in which it was made. I belief that, very few inventions or innovations are made in laboratories, and most of them have occurred when we look closely at the problems and nature that are happening around us. In that sense, at the lowest cost, in the simplest possible way, if my innovation is a global achievement, then why would I call this simply as Innovation? It would not be an exaggeration to say that has earned me the name of "People's Scientist" among the people, it's my "A Compact Tool that diagnoses Eight diseases".

Purpose of the Invention:

It was schooling days. I was studying in 3rd standard in a Government aided school located in a small village named as Pattiveeranpatty. My class teacher Shri. Krishnamoorthy told me that "Ayyappan You will become a Scientist One day" after an interesting incident happen in the class room. Yes, that has become my DREAM. My childhood dream is to become a Scientist.

After great struggle but with lots of interest and involvement, I have become a Scientist at CSIR. My next dream was to receive the award in the name of the great Scientist, my inspiring role model, the Nobel Laurette Sir C.V. The dream of receiving an award in the name of CV Raman prevailed, from the news learned through the internet, from those who succeeded in the invention or innovations related to light. Knowing that the award is also being given in the name of CV Raman, I continued my efforts in doing research in the field of Light.

Unexpectedly, my father was suffering from heart problem and he was admitted to a private hospital in Chennai for the treatment. He was diagnosed with Triple Valve block and advised to undergo Open-Heart bypass surgery. The surgery was completed within two weeks of time and he was admitted to the intensive care unit.(ICU)

In just two days, the doctors diagnosed that my father might have Jaundice and asked him to get a blood test done immediately. I went to the bill counter for making payment for the blood test. Immediately the person at the counter said, "Give me Six thousand rupees (Rs. 6,000/-)." I was totally shocked and surprised. Thinking that he was probably saying something wrong, I asked once again, "How much should I pay?" And again, he said very clearly, "Six thousand rupees" to me.

I was really shocked, confused and got annoyed. "I do not understand, Six thousand rupees for a normal blood test?" I said. He replied that "Yes. Your father has been admitted to the intensive care unit (ICU). That's why it's so much money."

"What is this non-sense. You people are cheating. Because a person admitted in ICU, you may charge whatever you feel like. This is too much and It's unfair," I said innocently. I got angry and replied to the counter person very harshly. He replied, "Okay. You go and check out with PRO (Public Relation Officer). He himself will explain to you." I also immediately went to see the PRO.

That PRO is the one who has opened my eyes of knowledge. It would not be an exaggeration to say why he was even a tool for this invention to happen. His explanation made me to understand. The first question he asked me was; "What work are you doing?". I replied, "I am a Scientist in the Central Government's Research Organization." He replied, "I think I'm talking to the right person." Then he continued his explanation.

Bacteria are a microorganism that is invisible to one's eyes. Its size is just the size of the nanometer or the picometer(10^{-9} to 10^{-12} meter). You can't see with your nacked or bare eyes. Pathogen or Bacterial Detection cannot be detected even by a microscope. That's why, they use the other method called "Culture Test". In this method, the blood sample is placed in an incubator.

An incubator is a device used to grow and maintain microorganisms or cells. The incubator maintains optimum temperature, humidity and other conditions such as the CO_2 and oxygen content of the sample kept inside.

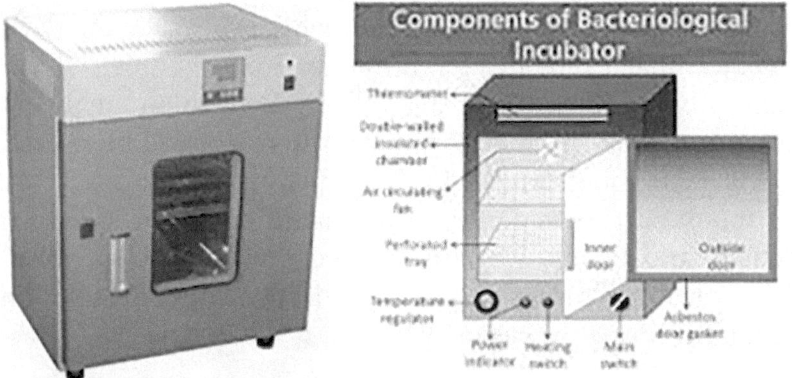

Incubator maintains the sample (blood) temperature condition similar to body condition and keep agitating (rotation at constant speed). Proper food is also fed into the sample so that the microorganism to grow faster.

This process is extended till the bacteria grows to size larger than micron in size. Then the blood sample is stained on a glass plate and viewed under the microscope. With the help of a microscope, whether there are bacteria present or not can be detected. To detect the presence of bacteria in this method, it takes at least 36 hours to 48 hours. The PRO also explained that the cost would be less, which is why they charge between Rs. 200 and Rs. 300 for a normal blood test.

Let us assume the patient is admitted in ICU. Can you wait for 36-48 hours to find out whether the blood sample has a specific disease or not? What will happen if you just wait for 36-48 hours. At first, I realized that it was difficult. "So, is there no other way to do this?" I asked, and the respected PRO replied.

"Instead of a blood test called Culture Test, there is a technique called PCR (i.e. Polymeric Chain Reaction), which can be used to detect the presence or not of the disease within six hours. I think you know what is PCR technique? In Polymeric Chain Reaction method, the bacteria are not magnified; they are multiplied. One bacterium into 10 and keep multiplying by repeating the chain.

The cost of the PCR device ranges from around Rs 3 to Rs 4 crore. Because the device being highly expensive, the device will be available only in a few hospitals. From this hospital, your father's blood for a blood test will be taken in an ambulance, tested in a PCR machine there, and the report will be released. It will take about 6-8 hours. That's why this blood test costs six thousand rupees. Do you understand now?", he asked very politely and kindly. He also stressed that, "You also being a Scientist, Why don't you just try to come out with some solution," he said, arousing my curiosity.

Then I immediately went to the counter, paid the money, received the receipt, and rushed towards the blood test. After the test was over, fortunately, we brought my father home from the hospital without any problem and he is doing fine with God's grace.

Thought Flows:

But my thoughts did not stop. The desire to build such an instrument at a very low cost eventually became my dream. The aim of my research was to reduce the diagnostic time and reduce the cost of the diagnostic tool. Even though the diagnostic devices were in use in six hours, the cost of the device was in crores of rupees. We too have to build a diagnostic device in six hours at a cost of Rs 1.0 lakh. The dream was to make that invention for the benefit of the common people and the rural people. I started this research work full-heartedly. Wherever you go and whatever you see, it's the same dream. The quest for how we were going to do this continued.

As said by Swami Vivekananda, "Take up one Idea as your Goal. Make that Idea as life. Let the brain, muscle, nerves and every part of your body lives on that Idea. Live on it. Dream on it. This is the way to Success." Yes. I realised the impact this statement in my life.

One day, I had gone to Thiruvanmiyur beach in Chennai for fun with my family. It was a beautiful evening. It was time for the sunlight to begin to fade. Sitting on the beach sand, chewing on snacks, eyes wandering here and there. The waves were like a little child, coming and touching the shore, and getting tired again without a mind. Here and there, the children were running and playing kabaddi and playing ball in the soil.

The Senior-Citizens and married couples were talking about their past stories. Some lovers did not know what the culture was, and without bothering about others sitting nearby, they were teasing and throwing the sea away.

Even at that time, sitting next to my wife, my thinking was moving towards my dream. I can hear my wife wailing, "Hey, you have come to the beach to enjoy with the family. But you are always thinking something else. What's wrong with you?"

At the distance of around 100 meters, a toy and balloon seller was blowing colored balloons for the children and selling. That's where my research started. There was nothing to be seen in the balloon that had not been blown. But when the fellow started blowing the balloon, I know that something is written on it. Those letters "Happy Birthday" on the fully blown balloon catch my eye. One more thing came to my eyes. On that dim evening, the question arises in me as to how the letters "Happy Birthday" written on the balloon are so vivid. Yes. The letters are written in shimmering ink called "Fluorescence." Virtually, I just got up and said, "Eureka... "Eureka" and feel like shouting.

Yes, those characters that are not visible to the eyes at first are the bacteria I am looking for in my invention. This unblemished balloon is the blood cells that carry those bacteria. So far, we have been able to detect the bacteria through a microscope, let the bacteria grow and wait until their size becomes larger. Instead, when we use this new "Fluorescence-based Pathogen Detection" method, we will soon be able to detect the presence of bacteria.

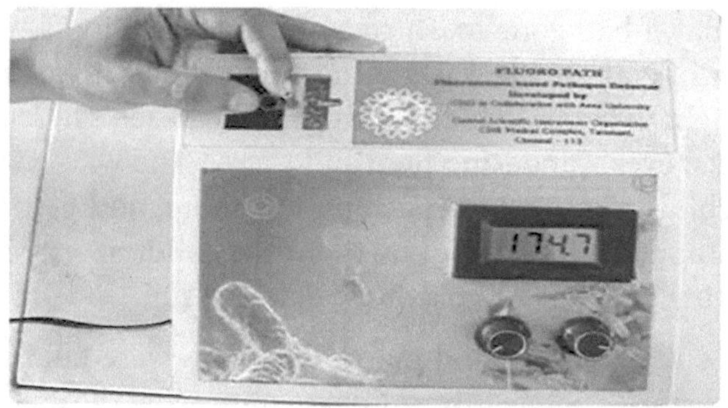

The result of this invention was a diagnostic tool called "Fluropath" at a cost of Rs. 30,000. Diagnosis in just 4-6 hours from the time of blood transfusion. Using the tool is a very simple way. Diagnosis at a very low cost. So far, chikungunya, typhoid and Dengue are the eight types of diseases that can be detected in a single device. The award given to me by the Government of India for this is "Sir.C.V. Raman" award.

Shall we see how this tool works? Even if it is a little difficult, if you try to understand, you will definitely understand. Take a good look at the picture given below.

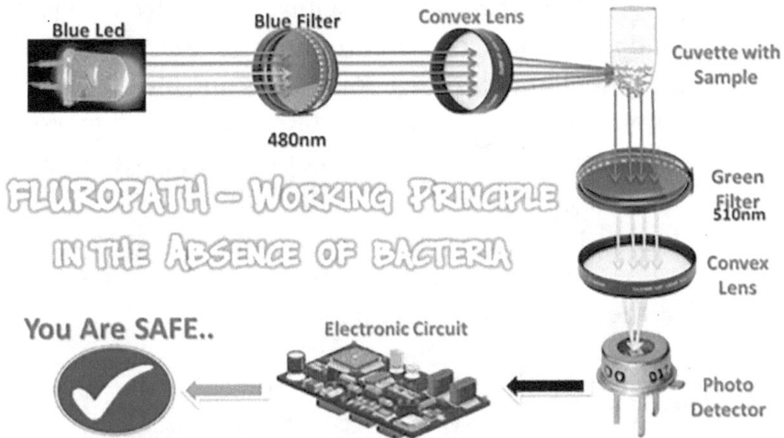

Let me first explain very easily how this tool works. The blood to be tested should be taken in a 2-3 ml glass cuvette and mixed with a luminous fluorophore called antigen and kept in the incubator for 6-8 hours. The glass cuvette should be taken and placed in the appropriate place in the diagnostic device and covered.

Now when the blue colored light is injected into it, if there are no bacteria in the blood being examined, the dark bluelight will penetrate and come out as dark bluerays. In other case, the dark bluerays are absorbed and released as green light rays.

This is the basic principle of this tool, and the uniqueness and specialty of this invention is that it is made entirely from products available in our country and at a very low price.

First, let's assume that the blood being tested does not contain bacteria. Generally, when light is emitted in a blue LED, the light emits a variety of light rays such as dark blue, blue, purple, etc., i.e. Colors Near Blue. We need only certain purple lasers to detect bacteria more accurately, especially an optical filter that transmits only 480 nm of light rays.

These light rays are then focused on a convex lens and concentrated on a glass cuvette containing the blood to be examined. Those rays illuminate the fluorophore in the glass cuvette. According to the above principle, if there are no bacteria in the blood examined, the Fluorophore in the glass cuvette absorbs the blue light and then emits the same blue light. This blue light is passed through the green filter; hence no light comes out from the green filter. So, no rays of light will come out. As a result, no change will be made to the light detector or photo detector placed there. It is detected through a microcontroller and program and on the display "YOU ARE SAFE" – which means that there is no bacterial impact.

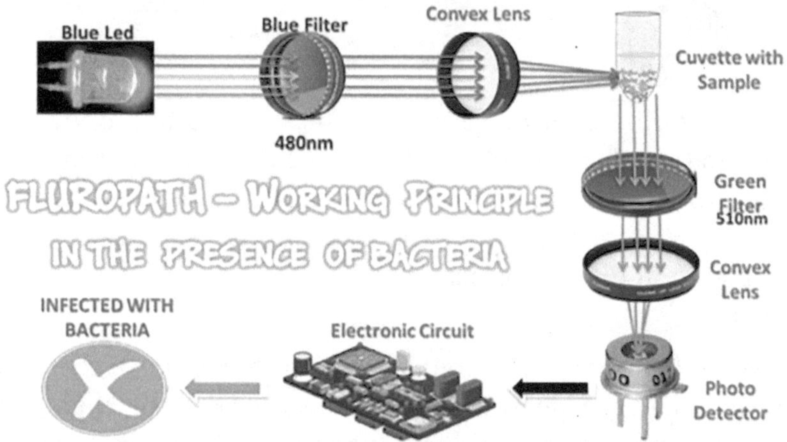

Now let's look at the second phase. That is, let's say that the blood being tested contains bacteria. According to the foregoing theory, if the blood examined contains bacteria, the Fluorophore in the glass cuvette absorbs the blue light and emits green light. The emitted rays contain a variety of green rays. When they pass through the green filter, only 510 nm of green rays are allowed. Those rays are perceived in the light detector or photo detector placed there and transmit the current through it through the installed microcontroller and program. Detected and displayed on the display "YOU ARE INFECTED" – which means it is confirmed that there is an impact of bacteria.

The diagnostic tools available so far, whether there are bacteria or not? It can only be discovered. It only QUALIFIES. This means that whether it is chikungunya/viral fever or any other disease, it can only be ascertained whether "YES or NO" - "POSITIVE or NEGATIVE". But, in this finding, it not only determine whether the bacteria are present or not, but also to realize the extent to which the bacteria affected. Not only Qualifying; also Quantifying. It is not an exaggeration to say that it is used to cure patients easily. Not only that, the device is also capable of detecting eight types of diseases at the same time.

The invention occurred in 2009. After nearly 4 years of intensive testing, the device was released with medical clearance. The medical ethical committee has also recommended that the reliability of the device is 99.7%. Among the medical devices worth Rs 3-4 crore, it should be developed within 6-8 hours at a cost of just Rs 30,000 and it should reach the public in every government hospital, government primary health centers, irrespective of urban and rural areas. In 2011, the Government of India awarded me an award for "Sir C.V. Raman" award. Among the people, among the students, the name I got was "People Scientist". The medals, awards and rewards given to me by scientific movements and intellectuals are many.

It would be an exaggeration to say to me on every platform, "Science is for the Good Cause i.e. Creation– not for the path of Destruction," and it is an exaggeration to say that this is a noble invention that made sense of its true meaning. I also understand that you who are reading these pages of this book are going to be inspired. I can feel you getting up from bed, straightening up, sitting down and reading with a sideways. Come on, let's take a look at our next mind-blowing invention!

❑

A DEVICE THAT AUTOMATICALLY PRESCRIBES THE DRUG

"Innovation requires an experimental mindset." - Denise Morrison

The third mind-blowing Innovation:

Another fascinating innovation that we will see next is a continuation of my earlier invention. The next inspiring innovation is titled, "Tool that automatically prescribes the drug". The alternate names given to this innovation are "Anti-Biogram" or "Multi-Drug Resistance System (MDR)". The explanations of it can be seen in great detail in this chapter. Are you ready, my friends?

Background of this innovation:

For example, let's assume we have fever. What shall we do first? Let's go and show it to the doctor. Will they give you medicines right away? No. First of all, they will ask few questions like "What did you eat? Did you eat something cool? Did you drink any safeless water you have come across?". He asks us a variety of questions and diagnosing your problems, such as symptoms.

If the mosquito bites and if there's a cold fever late in the evening, it could be malaria. If the body hurts so badly or painful, may be it's a viral fever. If diarrhea or vomiting continues than the root cause may be food poison, in all the cases, Doctor suggest for a blood test or urine test.

Then the patient should be taken to the clinical lab or diagnostic lab, where do they give blood or urine for the test and after 36-48 hours, you will get the report. If it comes to "Negative" in the experiment, you can't think of saying "Oh. I am Safe. Escaped!" The next step is to perform another test of whether there is some other disease, as we have seen earlier, this method is called a "culture test."

Let's assume the blood test result shows "Malaria is Positive", then take the confirmed test report to the doctor. The doctor will give a surprising look at you and say, "Very Bad. You got infected by Malaria", and he would give a reaction, as something that should not come to you at all. He would immediately ask, "Do you have any medication allergies?". Then he will prescribe a medicine from a number of medicines made for malaria, that too from certain medicines that are readily available in the local medical shop supplied by the medical representatives.

This can be continued if the fever subsides. Otherwise, you can consider some other medicine alternatively. This is called a "Course of Medicine". The doctors cannot be blamed for this. When two people have the same disease, the medicine prescribed for one person may have worked well, but the same medicine may not work for another person. The blood is different. The amount of immunity in the blood may change, the nature or severity of the disease may be different. That is not to say that the medicine that worked for me did not work for another person. It can cause and cause side effects. Sometimes it can even be life-threatening.

By keeping these problems in mind, I have innovated a simple mechanism or tool that could prescribes medicines automatically. You know one thing; I have designed and fabricated this entire unit with the help of waste materials available from metal scrapes from old shops. The device that is shown in the figure below is the one that automatically prescribes the medicines that were produced in its first structure, which is capable of operating with the help of a computer.

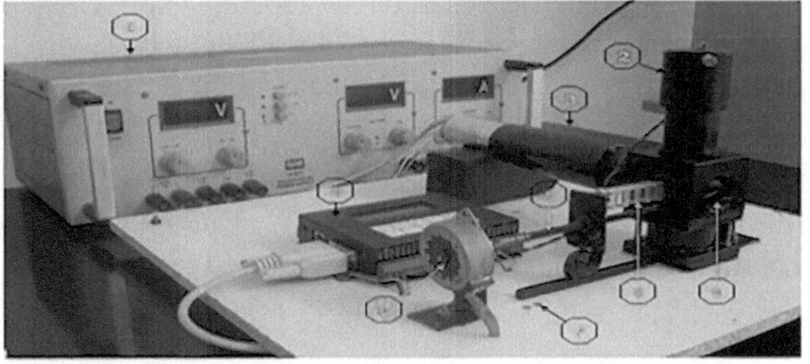

How the tool works:

Let's take a look at how this tool works. In this tool, 12-glass cuvette strips are used in an interconnected position, as shown in the image below, just as a glass cuvette was used in the "Fluropath" tool. That cuvette is coded from number one to twelve. In the first cuvette, just distilled water is poured. 2-3 ml of confirmed infected blood is filled from cuvette 2 – 12 cuvettes. Different anti-biotics for that particular disease with different dosages are put on the cuvettes coded from 2 to 11. It is also named AB1-AB10. In the 12th cuvette, we don't add any anti-biotics; which contains only infected blood and does not include any medication. The first cuvette is determined to be 0% (and named as Blank) and the 12th cuvette is determined to be 100% (Control). Necessary food is added to the blood sample for the microorganism to grow faster and kept in an incubator for about 2-3 hours.

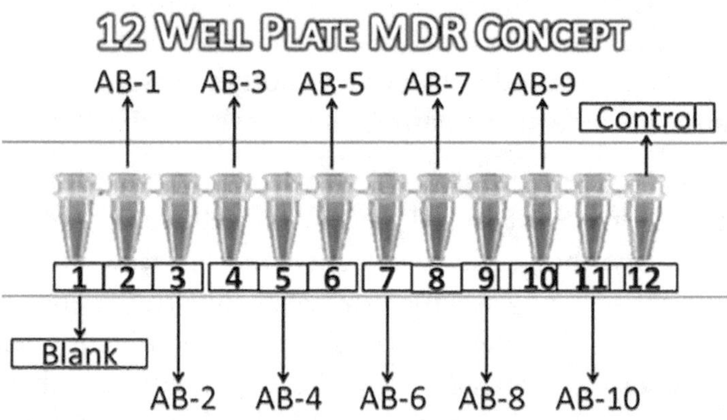

Suppose that normal fever has been detected in the tested blood, anti-biotics such as paracetamol, crocin, Dola, etc., should be given to each cuvette at doses of 250, 500, 650 dose-wise. It is not mandatory to put blood and medicines in all the cuvettes. Here, after 2-3 hours kept in the incubator, the system should be attached to the testing machine.

This tool works in the same way that "Fluropath" works. Each time, a cuvette is checked. Each cuvetteis moved to the inspecting area through a stepper motor, most accurately, through a computer or microcontroller. In this way, all the 12 cuvettes are tested and the data is recorded.

It is only now that you need to understand one thing better. Do you remember what is the sign of a particular disease in the blood tested? Kindly try to recall from our previous chapter. Are you remembering? Correct. You have found out very correctly. "Green rays of light". Haven't we realized in the previous invention that if it is dark green, the impact or strength of the disease is greater and if it is light green in color, the impact of the disease is less.

We have filled all the cuvettes with blood infected with the same bacteria. If the medicines in each cuvette worked well, the green color would have been completely gone. If it had worked only somewhat, then it would be light green. If the medicine doesn't work at all, it'll be dark green, just like it's in the 12th cuvette, isn't it?

The recorded data are calculated by the computer, fixing the water in the first cuvetteas 0%, and the blood sample in the 12th cuvette as 100%, changing the green color from 2nd to 11th cuvettes are mapped to 0-100%. Then the data from 0-30% is called SENSITIVE medicine, and 30-70% is represented as INTERMEDIATE medicine and 70-100% of the data into RESISTANCE to react. Look at the picture given below. You will understand. The computer prepares a report on its own, selects and prints out the correct medicine for a particular person, for a particular disease, and according to its condition, and gives a report on the correct medicines to be prescribed by the doctor.

This innovation suggests that if the right medicine is chosen, the disease will also be cured and there will be no side effects. NO MORE TRIAL AND ERROR TREATMENT. How do you rate this innovation that supports doctors? Are you surprised? Isn't that Inspired? This one innovation is proof that if WE THINK - WE CAN, it will be fulfilled. Yes, another award that I got for this innovation was the Bharath Ratna Dr. APJ Abdul Kalam Gold Medal Award. It was a private research and charitable organization that honored me with this prestigious award.

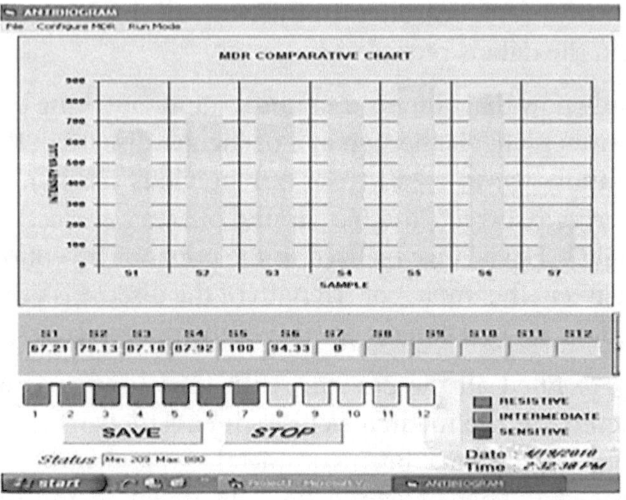

Hello friends! Are you very curious to know about the next invention or innovation? Don't you feel like continue reading this book? I am able to read your mind-voice saying with curiosity, "What Next?". What could be the fourth fascinating invention will be." Who am I to hinder your curiosity? Here is the next inspiring invention/ innovation.

SOLAR POWERED VACCINE COOLER

"There is no innovation and creativity without failure." - *Brene Brown*

The fourth mind-blowing Innovation:

As we'll see next, another inspiring innovation of mine is the "Cooler that protects vaccines". The name given to this particular innovation is "Solar Powered Vaccine Cooler". In this section, problems and side effects of conventional vaccine coolers that have been in use for many decades are explained. I have explained about the device, which is being developed at a very low cost, preventing wastage of medicines, and which will soon come out as a life saving noble tool.

Even this innovation, I would regard it as an innovation that affected me to a great extent, for I would say that this innovation was a blessing to me, who was so obsessed with doing something for the common people. The way this innovation was made is a great story. As soon as I said Story; You are all excited. Well. Friends! Are you ready? Are you ready? YES. I am listening your mind-voice – "YES".

If the problem statement is defined and shaped first, then you will find a way to research. Then you will get a solution to the problem. What's that problem? In this chapter, I will also explain very easily how do we find a solution for it. A good friend of mine was the root cause of this innovation.

What's the problem?

It's something you know everything about. "Polio drops". "India along with 10 other countries in the South East Asian region of the World Health Organization (WHO) was declared

Polio-Free in 2014. No new cases of polio have been reported in India since January 2011. There is no evidence of the spread of VDPVs," the official report said.

It is not an exaggeration to say that the "Rotary Club" is credited with being the backbone of the government and executing the project so perfectly to say that "Today, No Polio in our country". Every time the polio drops are administered, my habit is to call every friend on the phone and tell them not to forget to put it on your children.

Let me explain about what is vaccine and how vaccination helps protecting us from any disease. Vaccine is nothing but a virus, for which we are fighting against that virus. Let us consider Co-Vaccine is nothing but injecting or vaccinating corona virus into our body with the controlled environment.

When the vaccine temperature is maintained between from 2°C to 6°C, then the virus is said to be Constructive Virus. When this virus is injected into our body, this help to build resistance power to fight against the disease and creates an immunity with in your body. Occasionally when that virus or bacteria try to attack us, the resistance power or immunity will fight against it and destroy it. This is what is called "Picking up a thorn with a thorn."

If the temperature of the vaccine exceeds beyond from 6°C and less than 8°C, it becomes dead virus. Only distilled water. No effect on virus. When the temperature exceeds from 8°C, it become destructive virus and becomes poisonous.

Now you have to pay close attention. Normally these vaccines are distributed through the small cooler box from village to village, street to street and distribute it to schools, colleges, railway stations, bus-stands and everywhere, thinking that it will be useful to the common public. The cooler is filled with nitrogen ice cubes, processed ice packets, or as a gel. Within two hours of taking, the temperature of the vaccine rises. Sometimes, the ice cubes melt and even become water. Its temperature is about 10°C or beyond this. Are we putting the vaccine afterwards? We give only water or sometimes poison to children and adults.

Understanding this problem, I used to call my friends over the phone and said, "Don't get vaccinated wherever it is available. You may kindly take your kids to a good government or private hospital and go to places where there is a freezer facility and get vaccinated. Even if the private hospitals ask for money for it, kindly PAY for it and get them vaccinated. In my opinion, only then will we get the full benefit of getting vaccinated. My friends also understood it they tried to followed what I said.

Innovative Idea:

I have been saying the same thing for more than two years. One of my friends suddenly started scolding me. "You keep talking about this issue for many years. Don't you have any other work to do? We are all fellow human beings, ordinary people. But you are a Scientist. You are saying that you have to do something for this country and the common people. Can't you do anything about it?" My friend said. It was as if I was being slapped.

I concluded that we somehow had to find a cooler that would carry a vaccine without any refrigerants, works on the battery, especially at a lower cost. It turned into a DREAM, almost three-and-a-half years of hard work, not hard work, very hard work, dedicated, sleepless, and work as a team.

We implemented this project together as a team. This was aided by the government itself with the necessary financial assistance and supports. I did not prepare any presentations to explain the project to the government, but on the contrary, I explained it only with the picture shown below, and the project was immediately approved.

Cooler that Protects Vaccines:

Do you understand the description of the project? Give it a try. If you can't, I'll explain myself. Sun, light, energy, portable, cooler, vaccine bird. I think you can connect now. Yes, a Portable, Solar-Powered Vaccine Cooler that can be easily transported, solar powered, and carrying vaccines.

We know that any cooler or AC works on chemical refrigerant like freon. Many refrigerant systems work on the principle of Thermodynamic Reverse Rankine Cycle. When any gas is compressed it produces heat. All gases are having positive temperature coefficient. As you compress, heat will be produced as per Boyle's law. (PVT relationship). When volume if compressed at constant pressure, the temperature of the gas will increase. For example, when you fill the air with cycle pump. There is a piston; when it is push it, it compresses the air and get filled in the type tube. Because of this reason, you may observe that heat will be released.

But some of the gases are called the Noble gases or inert gases, possess opposite property. When they are compressed, the temperature will decrease. This is the phenomenon is employed in the air-conditioner and coolers.

But in this innovation, there is no coolant; no refrigerant. It employs the effect of "Peltier effect." The innovated Solar Powered Vaccine Cooler is been visualized in three images as shown below:

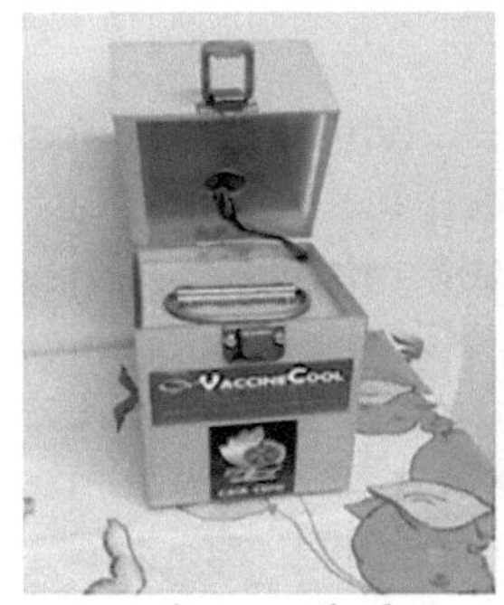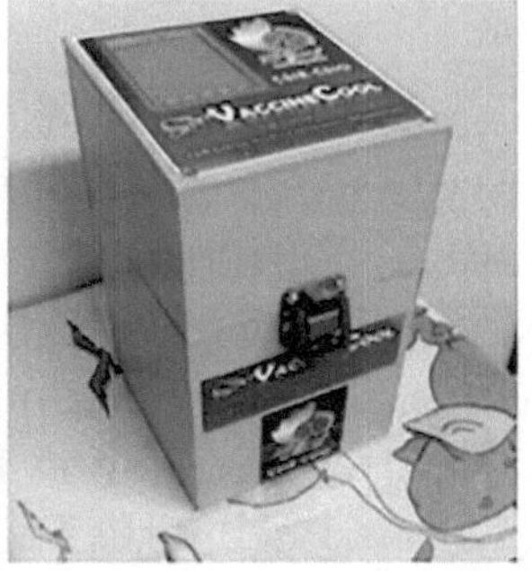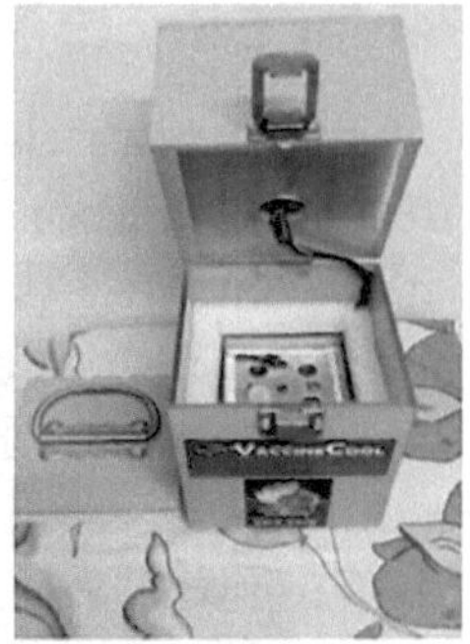

We learned about the reason for the innovation. We enjoyed the innovation as well. It must be called innovation rather than invention. There are two people behind this inspiring innovation, none other than Seebeck and Peltier. Now I think you're curious to know how it works. Come on, let's read. Let's see.

Seebeck Effect:

When two dissimilar metal wires are joined together to form two junctions, and if one junction say "A" is kept in ice-bath i.e. cold and the other junction named "B" is kept in hot water, then an emf will be produced across the junctions. This emf is called as "thermo-emf". This is due to thermal gradients created across the junction. This effect is called "Seebeck Effect", and invented by a Scientist ThomasJohan Seebeck.

The Seebeck effect was used in thermocouple, which is used for the temperature measurement applications. When a greater number of thermocouples are connected in series or parallel, it can be named as thermopiles, which can be used to generate electricity mainly in the satellite applications.

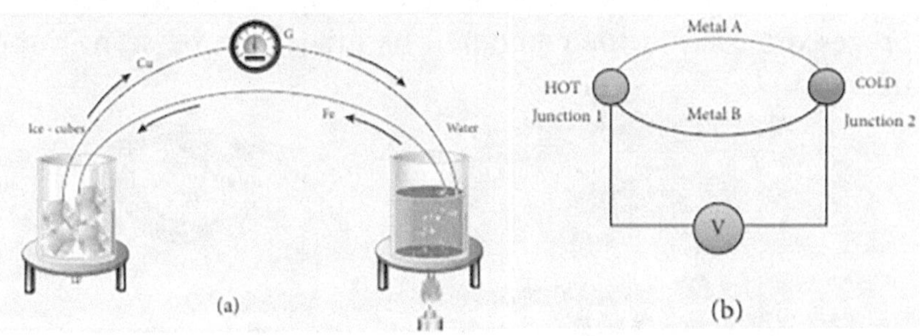

Peltier Effect:

Later a physicist named Peltier, while studying the Seebeck effect in the laboratory, accidentally replaced the galvanometer with a battery by mistake. The result of the mistake is a new invention. Yes. Researcher Learn from their failure or experience. The terminal on the ice, i.e., the junction, revealed heat. As a result, the ice began to melt. The boiling water began to freeze. Realizing this, Peltier also named it the Peltier effect.

When an electric current is passed through a circuit of a thermocouple, heat is generated at one junction and absorbed at the other junction. This is known as the Peltier effect: the presence of heating or cooling at an electrified junction of two different conductors. The effect is named after French physicist Jean Charles Athanase Peltier, who discovered it in 1834. When a current is made to flow through a junction between two conductors, A and B, heat may be generated or removed at the junction.

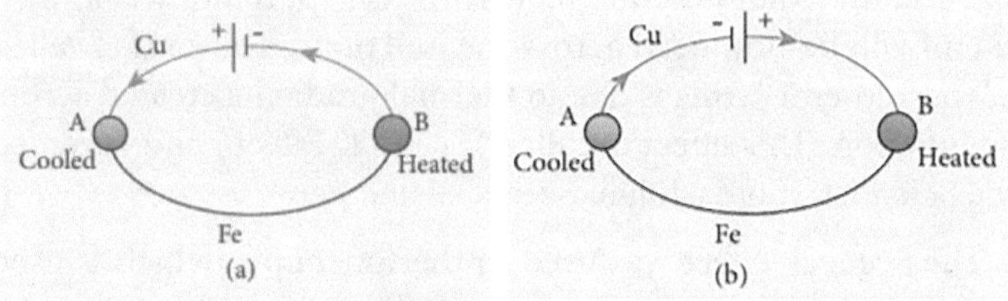

There was no application for the use of Peltier effect. In 1970s, due to the invention of the semiconductor devices, in the name of Thermo-Electric Module (TEM) or Thermo-Electric Couple (TEC) were developed and used Cooling device for Pentium processors used in the computer. Its model can be seen in the figure.

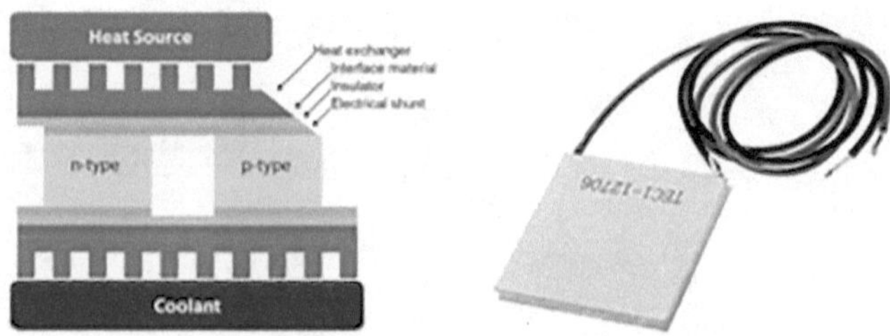

In the innovation of Solar-powered Vaccine Cooler, the TEC modules are used to produce the cooling effect to protect the vaccines. Its technique cannot be fully explained here because of the patent and copyright issues.

The person who is going to distribute the vaccine need to protected from the hot sun. To mitigate it, they will be given an umbrella. If the umbrella is opened, the solar panel printed on top of it, will generate electricity from the sun and there is also a USB connector on the handle of the umbrella. If we attach it to our cooling device as it is, the battery will automatically charge. So that the battery power will increase even more. This is also an achievement.

In conclusion, the "Solar-powered Vaccine Cooler" device developed as innovation costs just Rs 6,000. The medicine kept inside does not get spoiled; the cooler that protects the potency of the vaccine. So, at any time, you can take it and distribute the vaccine. As a result, the benefit of administering vaccine will increase manifold.

SMART VACCINE COOLER:

Now that IoT technology has become very widely used in the current era, I am making some innovations in my next venture. I will only describe here about some of its main features.

- This device can be handled; monitored; calculated through a centralized Surveillance System.

- Only in biometric mode, the device canbe opened and handled only by an authorized person.

- Inside and outside temperatures can be monitored and controlled by mobile or internet

- How many times, the device was opened; When was it closed; It will help to know more accurately

- How many people have been given the drug.

- The battery condition is monitored and advised.

- This cooling device is also designed with many more smart stuffs.

What friends! How was this Innovation? Upon hearing all this, do you feel the urge to achieve and find something? "What's the question? I can even hear you thinking in the mind voice, i.e., mentally, that it will definitely appear." It would not be an exaggeration to say that this innovation is also one of the reasons why people lovingly call me a "People's Scientist". What's right.

Okay. Come on, I understand that you're eager to know about the next mind-blowing invention/ innovation, even without eating, even without sleeping, and continuing without putting down this "Ten out of Ten" book.

❑

A WATER - POWERED MOTOR VEHICLE

"Innovation is the calling card of the future." - Anna Eshoo

The fifth mind-blowing Invention:

The next Innovation we are going to see is an Innovation that will amaze the whole world. Yes, a motor vehicle driven by water. Will the motor-bike run on water? Is it amazing? At first, I was surprised too. I was surprised at first, and I got good answers. Even as we were asking questions like Possible? Is it possible? The Inventor says, "Come on, let's go in that motor vehicle too." I'm ready. Are you ready?

About the Innovation:

A Brazilian inventor has developed a water-powered motorcycle that can travel up to 520 km (310 mile) in a liter of water, the inventor says. In order to save money on his daily commute, Ricardo Azevedo, with his 1993 Honda NX-200 motor. He modified the motorcycle to use water instead of petrol.

On February 7, 2016, Brazilian inventor Ricardo Acevedo invented and released a water-powered motorcycle. The

H_2O-powered super clean motorcycle has been invented. The motorcycle produces clean steam and can even be operated by contaminated sewage water. It is capable of travelling up to nearly 310 miles per liter of water. The vehicle is a combination of battery and fuel-cell; It is used to produce electricity and to separate hydrogen from water molecules.

Moto Power H2O:

He has named it as "Moto Power H2O". It breaks down the water molecules and converts them into oxygen and hydrogen. Hydrogen is released in large quantities and he uses this hydrogen to run the motorcycle engine. Ricardo Acevedo has modified his motorcycle to run it with water. He has also proved that hydrogen can be produced from water. Hydrogen molecule from the water; He demonstrates that when weeds are stuffed into a soap flask, water bubbles come out and explode when it is set on fire.

$$H_2O \rightarrow 2H^+ + O$$

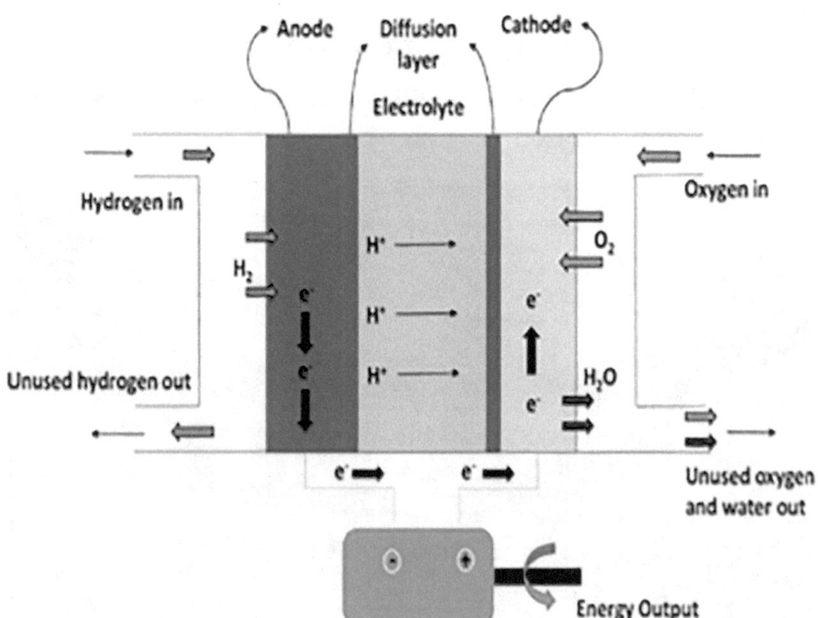

"This motorcycle runs on hydrogen extracted from water. And in the hybrid experimentThat I did, it could go at a speed of 520 km Per liter of water," says the creator proudly. Also, the motorcycle runs at a speed of 120 kmph without any vibration or noise.

Running in any water:

Some people expressed misconceptions about his Innovation; that is, he mixes some acid in the water, prepares it and puts it in the motorcycle tank. So that's why it's working. To make the people can feel and believe, he shows a motorcycle that runs in the water, first by drinking the water, and then putting the same water in his motorcycle tank, proving that the motorcycle runs on the water.

He first proved it with the most suitable distilled water; then, through his research, he took contaminated sewage water from the Tiete river, one of the world's most polluted rivers, and filled it on his motorcycle and proved that it works best. Surprisingly, the inventor said that the contaminated water of the Tite river also works for better water levels.

Can we drive too?

Have you seen, friends, in the midst of people wasting water, our Acevedo, who invented a motor vehicle that runs on water, is admirable! You put the water in the bike, it will just pick up the cart.

Yes, friends! Soon this motor vehicle will be available in our market as well. Surely, if you buy a motor vehicle that runs in this water and put one liter of water in it, i.e. put it in the cart and go for a round. How is it? Like you, I'm also waiting to get used to this cart. What a mind-blowing Innovation this is! Do you like it? Then come on, let's see about the next Innovation.

❏

SELF-PROPELLED AUTOMATIC WHEELCHAIR

"Without change there is no innovation, creativity, or incentive for improvement. Those who initiate change will have a better opportunity to manage the change that is inevitable." - William Pollard

The sixth mind-blowing Innovation:

Another heart-touchinginnovation that we're going to see as the sixth out of ten is the wonderful Innovation of one of my students, the "Automatic Wheelchair that runs on its own".

People's President, The Missile Man, A.P.J. Abdul Kalam Ji often says that, "Every Scientist should think that we have a greater responsibility to create Young Scientists and make them to become a Successful Scientist. Only then will our India become a Strengthened India." I am the one who straight away follows his concepts and walks as his shadow on the path he has shown to us.

Young Scientists:

Vowing to achieve and at the same time produce young successful scientists, I started spending at least 6-hours of interaction with students every week, on Saturdays and Sundays, which are weekends, at a government school in some rural town, on the topic "Thinking of becoming a Scientist – Ways & Means" and "Secret of Success (SoS)" and invite them to get motivated in studying science and creating the curiosity. Without imposing science, I develop an interest in them. I am helping them as much as possible to make them successful scientists as well.

In that way, I share with you the Innovation of our young scientists and little kalams, who are inspired by me, whose seeds of science have been sown, germinated into plants, bumped into their knees, and are growing and achieving fruit as a fruit-bearing tree today. It is a matter of pride to think that I have produced six young scientists in that way. It's a lot of proudness. Let me introduce some of my followers as Young Scientists.

Krithik Vijayakumar is a young storm. He met me when he was in the ninth grade. He completed class XII in 2023. As on today, he holds 12 national level awards, 8 state-level awards, young scientist award, young entrepreneur award. Yes. He is the Director and CEO of the company "Futuro Robotics". The wisdom of teaching robotics technology even to college students. Last year, he was also awarded the "Young Award Scientist" award by our Trust.

The next Young Scientist, World record holder. Thirumuruga Veerabahu has made it to the list of the world's top 20 innovators. When he was studying in the post-graduate engineering department, he joined me as a project student. He was awarded a national-level award for his invention. Once the award is received, a call from Japan, a call from Germany came. But my student, my disciple, brushed it all aside and started a self-employment on his own with the dream of "I have to do something for my motherland", and gave it the name "Cybernoid Technologies" and today Thirumuruga Veerabahu is the man who is emerging as an accomplished hero, a young scientist.

In this chapter, we are going to look at his first innovation, that is, that national award-winning innovation. Yes, "Self-driving Automatic Wheel-Chair". This Innovation helps a person who had a stroke or rheumatoid arthritis to move through a wheelchair without the help of joystick or navigation buttons.

In this chapter, we will see in great detail the explanations and the root cause of the innovation, the manner in which the innovation was created, and its application. Are you ready, my friends?

My disciple Thirumuruga Veerabahu was doing his Master's degree in Engineering in Embedded Systems and Controls from

Anna University. He came to me and said,"Sir. I have to do a project only with you. That too, we have to create something innovative and good for the benefit of this society," I said, "Okay. If that is the case, then you have to bring a societal important problem statement."

He said, "Okay Sir", and after almost a week, he came to me and said, "Sir. I don't find any problems that are significant." I was amazed and asked Veerabahu, "What? You don't find any problem. Do you think, the Universe has become problemless? Well, where did you search for the problem?" I asked, to which Veerabahu replied, "I searched the website on Google, sir."

I replied, "We should not look for the problems from the Google. Each one of us will have a variety of problems and they are always unique in nature. For everyone around us, there will be at least ten problems. In every house, for every mother, how many problems will there be. Especially how many problems in the kitchen?". Veerabahu understood this and said, "Sir, what should I do now?"

Then he himself said, "Sir, I know a person is suffering from paralysis attack and is bedridden. He cannot do anything on his own. He can't even run a wheelchair?". I replied saying that, "In that case, at least, you should meet twenty-thirty people suffering from paralysis. I hope if you ask them a few questions and find out how they respond to your questions, there will be some way out". He too said "yes" and went on to meet more than 20 people suffering from paralysis and rheumatoid arthritis, interact with them and record video how they expressed their feelings.

After some time, we met and started watching the videos that were shot during the interactions held with affected patient. Almost everyone has answered "YES" or "NO" with their eye brows moving up and down and saying "yes", or "no" by frowning. When someone suffer from this disease, all the nerves in our body become paralyzed. Except the eyebrow veins located on the top of the eyes. We also discussed and confirmed with the doctors and then concluded that was the key feature of that innovation.

Normally, the wheelchair is controlled through buttons or joysticks, that makes the wheelchair to move forward or backward in an electric wheelchair. That's why this type of wheelchair could not be used by the paralyzed people without a supporting man-power. This invented wheelchair has no buttons or joysticks. The invented picked up a hat that everyone loved to wear. He placed two tactile sensors on the cap exactly where it touched the area above the two eyebrows. The cap is placed on the head of the patient.

The attached two sensors are connected to a micro-controller. In order to operate the right and left wheels of the wheelchair, two DC motors are connected. To control the two motors separately, two motor controllers were used and that too was attached to the micro-controller. The sensor senses the eyebrows moving up and down and the motors mounted on the wheel are turned on.

A total of five commands and related signal; The first command: To move both eyebrows up and down slowly, the wheelchair moves forward at a slower speed. The second command: To move both eyebrows up and down faster, the wheelchair moves forward at a slightly higher speed. Third command: When only the right eyebrow is moved, the wheelchair turns to the right. The fourth command: When only the left eyebrow is moved, the wheelchair turns to the left. The fifth command: If there is any problem, i.e., if the wheelchair approached staircase, steps or walls or in case of any emergencies, both eyes should be closed tightly, so that the wheelchair will stop abruptly with the help of magnetic brake and siren the emergency alarm.

If these five commands are taught or trained to a paralytic, if a bedridden person is made to sit in a wheelchair and put on the seat belt, the wheelchair can only be controlled by the movement of their eyebrows. The "self-propelled wheelchair" is a wonderful invention that travels around the house, sitting in a wheelchair and not lying in one place.

The "self-propelled wheelchair" won the first prize in state-level competitions. The invention has won the national award and awarded by the President of India; the great legend Dr. APJ. Abdul Kalam. Now this wheelchair is being developed in India and is being sold at a low cost for the benefit of the affected Indian people. What' s more, if this is my mind-blowing Innovation, it's a heart-threatening Innovation too.

❑

ANTI-PUNCTUREDVEHICLE TYRES

"Once you start innovating, KEEP innovating – make it too expensive for the competition to catch up." - Josh Chesney

The seventh Mind-Blowing Innovation:

Another fascinating Innovation that we are going to see next is "Anti-Punctured Vehicle Tyre". Yes, friends! This Innovation is such that under no circumstances will the tyres of the vehicle be punctured, even if the nail is pierced, the tyre will not burst, the vehicle will not derail and roll on the road, there will be no accidents, there will be no loss of life at all. If so, is it not a noble invention! In this chapter, we will see the explanations about it in great detail. What friends are you ready to travel in a vehicle that is not punctured at all? Let us travel together.

Doctoral Award for a School Dropout!

He was born on April 1, 1969, in Muthuramalingapuram village in Virudhunagar district. He was born as the son of Shri. Raman and Smt. Sangammal. His name is "Sealant Sekar". "Seland Sekar! What is that? We have heard that about the name "Dog Sekar" or "Blade Sekar" only in movies. What is that, "Sealant Sekar?". I understand that you are quite curious to know more about this "Sealant Sekar".

He was born into a very simple but poor family. While studying, he was trapped in the grip of poverty. To go to school, he walked almost 7 kilometer on foot even without a chapel. Perhaps that's why he doesn't like school. He doesn't like studying either. He studied till the third grade and also dropped-out. But he holds a Doctorate degree; Yes Doctorate; that is, Dr. Sekar. The doctorate degree was a reward for his Innovation.

The road accident that affected the mind!

He was just a school student. He had a very close family relative, i.e., his uncle. The uncle had travelled in a car from Virudhunagar to Chennai to attend a wedding ceremony with his family one day. The uncle had gone in the car with his wife and son. So, there are four people including the driver in total.

It was around two o'clock in the afternoon. As the car was passing through Trichy on bypass road, the front wheel of the car exploded with the sound of "Damal", the driver lost control, car rolled two to three times on the road, the truck carrying goods coming from behind the car got into it and the car crumbled like papads. Everyone in the car was hit hard. The driver and uncle died on the spot. The aunty also lost her life on the way to the Trichy hospital, carrying her wife and son in an ambulance. His son also died after being admitted to emergency treatment for three days.

It was only when he came to know how the accident took place that it was a big blow to the young Sekar. Well yes. A huge nail lying on the road pierced the tyre of a speeding car and the tyre exploded immediately. This incident is etched in the mind of our Sekar Ayya. "Can't we make a wheel, a tyre, that is not punctured at all? or Even if it's punctured, can't the vehicle run without any problems? Our Sekar Ayya has asked himself many times the same questions. In course of time, that became his Idea; Idea became the Goal; then the Goal became a Dream.

The Dream blossoms:

Over a period of time, he worked in many places. He worked hard and hard. One day he asked himself, "How long I will be Servant? Oneday I must become the boss. In a zeal to give jobs to four people, he runs an Exide battery and inverter company called SS Agencies in Thirumangalam, near Madurai. Under his administration, the company had grown very well, but he could never forget the accident that had entered his mind when he was a child and the cause of the accident.

That's why he started exploring a lot. He not only explored the national level; he started exploring the international level, how they are managing with this issue of tyre puncturing. Even if he found any chemical, he would buy it right away. If there were seminars on road safety or life saving devices on the road, he would immediately go and attend it. He would listen to anybody for clearing his doubts without any hesitation. Sometimes he would say, "Find something to keep the wheels of the vehicle away from getting punctured itself."

This continued for a long time. Once, he saw an advertisement from a foreign company. "Fill our chemical inside the tyre of the vehicle. This chemical will protect your tyre against punctured". Out of curiosity, he immediately bought the chemical, a foreign invention, and examined it. He also hoped that if the chemical was filled inside of the tube or the tubeless tire, it would not be punctured. But that effort did not yield as much complete success as expected.

At first, he began to study the chemical and its nature, which came from the foreign Innovation. One by one, he explored the problems and side effects of using the chemical.

The first problem: the chemical has to be replaced once in three to four months. The second problem is: if the temperature of the chemical inside the tyre goes up, sometimes the chemical will also burn and the tyre will burn. The third problem is: once the chemical inside becomes solidified, chemical changes take place, causing the tyre rim to rust. He listed about 10 such problems. In order to solve those problems, he began his research. He worked hard and hard. He put maximum effort; continuous effort; and constant effort. He persevered until he reached his goal and marched towards his dream.

The special features of the Innovation are:

He worked hard for almost eight years. Lots of obstacles. Despite all this, he made a wonderful, noble life-saving Innovation of his, and named as SSS, known as the SS Sealant, which we can shortly call as 3S. He also named it as Anti-Puncture Solution. He made the sealant by combining some chemical substances to form it, which cannot be explained very clearly because of patent and copyrights issues.

How to use the sealant:

- This chemical looks like rose milk.

- Our Sealant Sekar says that chemical can also be used on a tube tyre or a tubeless tyre.

- This sealant can be used for bicycles, two-wheelers (bikes or scooters), three-wheelers (autos), four-wheelers (cars, jeeps), six-wheelers (buses, lorries), heavy vehicles, tractors, Wheel loader, etc. So far, the sealant has been tested on all vehicles except aero-plane. Victory is the only word, he started listening.

- The sealant should be filled in the tyre of the vehicle. You don't need a large tool to fill. A one-feet-long plastic tube and an air-blowing cycle pump are enough, says its inventor. If it is a three or four or six-wheeler, a car or truck jockey will also be required to facilitate lifting that wheel slightly higher.

- First, they slowly lower the air from the tyre, fix the rubber tube in the sealant can, and fix the other side of it in the mouth of the wheel.

- Then, in the sealant tin, they pinch a needle. They then put it in the cycle pump and slowly hit the pump. The sealant chemical slowly spreads gradually into the interior of the tyre or tube. In case of a two-wheeler, 500 ml of sealant should be applied to both the wheels. In case of a car, 400 ml per tyre. On account of that, 2 liters are required for stepney as well.

- Once the sealant is fully filled, then air is loaded onto the wheel. Checking the air pressure and the work ends with this.

- When the vehicle is driven for up to a few meters, the sealant inside the tyre forms a layer inside around the tyre.

- Accidently, if a nail or any metal pin is pierced, the chemical on the inside, due to tyre pressure, immediately closes the hole. Even if the nail is on the tyre, the air does not descend. Even if the nail is removed, the sealant itself closes the hole. This process is called as Self-Healing.

The salient features of the 3 S-Innovation are as follows:

- If the big nail pierces the tyre, or if the tyre climbs onto the metal pin or rod, and if the pierced nail is still in the tyre; The tyre of the vehicle will not be punctured. The air on the tyre does not subside at all.

- This sealant helps to keep the tyre pressure steady. This increases the mileage of the vehicle. Up to 5% of fuel is saved, says the inventor of this sealant.

- The life span of the tyre increases by 25 per cent to 30 per cent, he says.

- Since the sealant for the tyre looks like a coolant, the heat of the road does not come into the tyre. So, the tyre does not catch fire.

- Similarly, the inventor describes the many aspects and uses of the sealant.

How I got impressed with 3S?

What is this? Is this Ayyappan saying something as if he had seen from its origin of the innovation? I understand what you're asking. As Tamil Poet Thiruvalluvar, who wrote 1330 Thirukkural, "Though things diverse from divers sages' lips we learn; The wisdom's part in each the true thing to discern In short, "To discern the truth in everything, by whomsoever spoken, is wisdom." One should not blindly accept whatever is heard from the word of mouth from anyone; One should enquire and realize the truth.

We invited this inventor, Dr. Sekar, as a special guest in a government school, for a programme called "Meet the Innovator" and asked him to talk about his Innovation.

At that time, I said, "If what you are saying is true, can you fill this sealant in my Maruti Alto-800 car and test it." Right away, a teacher stood up and asked "Can you please check on my two-wheeler as well?" He said, "So far, we have done such experiments in a lot of places. This is nothing new to us," he admitted.

Immediately, the team accompanying him brought the sealant and the necessary equipment. The team completed the work in less time, that is, within half an hour. Then, now we're going to find out and prove how this sealant works."

At first, they measured and noted the air pressure of the front and rear wheels of the two-wheeler. Then they placed a board in front of the two wheels. Oh! Three of the sharpest 4-inch nails on each board. They just moved the vehicle on top of the nail and lowered it. Immediately, they started driving. They went a couple of kilometers and then came back. A total of 4 kilometers. Again, they measured the air pressure on the tyre. The air pressure has not decreased at all. What is understood from this is that the six nails are pierced and the wheels are not punctured.

The same tests were performed on my car next. Now third year is running. To date, no wheel has been punctured. So far, even where the petrol bunk, if you measure the air pressure, you will say, "Sir. It's all right."

Award Sekar:

He has also been granted a patent for this invention. His invention was honored by the Government of Tamil Nadu and was awarded by the Governor of Tamil Nadu. The Academy of Universal for Global Peace was amazed by his Innovation and honored him with a Doctorate on Social Science, i.e., a doctorate who had studied only up to third grade. Here are some of the awards he received for his invention. "Peace Educator", "Mayan Award", "Innovative Product Award" and many more.

Once, when I met him, on behalf of our "Sow and Grow Teachers' Forum" and asked him "Why not You to be a mentor to the budding students and young budding Scientists", Dr. Sekar said politely, "Sir, if you lead the way, I will definitely do it."

At our request, he visits a lot of schools in today's times and gives enthusiastic speeches to students, explains his invention and sows the seeds of science in students. In appreciation of his Innovation and service, he was awarded the "Kalam Scientist Award" in 2022 on behalf of our "Sow and Grow Teachers' Forum". You will ask why in the name of Kalam. It was Kalam Ayya who fully realized that science is the path of creation and not the path of destruction. We are the ones who follow him and that is why the award is in his name.

His invention is very popular in the state of Andhra Pradesh, and beyond Tamil Nadu. Very often he says, "Andhra Pradesh and Telangana that give me the bread and butter" as a gratitude. His invention is now heating up in Tamil Nadu as well.

What friends! This sealant is also a mind-blowing invention with the motto of "Punchureless vehicle wheels - accident-free roads - life-free travel". Dr. Sekar Ji is an uneducated genius. He changed the trend that one can achieve only by studying and showed that anyone can achieve it. Friends, are you also ready to buy SS Sealant and use it in your vehicle? I wish you all the very best for your journey to be an accident-free journey and a comfortable journey. Would you recommend this Innovation to your friends as well? Come on, let's see the next fascinating Innovation. Come on.

❑

URINE-POWERED ELECTRICITY GENERATOR

"For good ideas and true innovation, you need human interaction, conflict, argument, debate." - Margaret Heffernan

The eighth mind-blowing Innovation:

"The urine-powered electricity generator" – the Innovation of four Nigerian school girls in Africa is another heart-touching and inspiring Innovation that we're going to see next." Urine… Cheechi… What are you talking about, sir?"; but the four young girls say "NO"; The Innovation of these young scientists is a rare lesson; A lesson for all of us.

Many school students get shy when I talk about this Innovation or urine on a lot of platforms. Because that's how we created them. We have instilled in the students, even in small children, an idea that even talking is wrong. That is what has become predominant in their mind. You have to realize that "None of the creations created by Nature are in vain." Even waste can be converted into energy, money. Yes. Waste to Wealth.

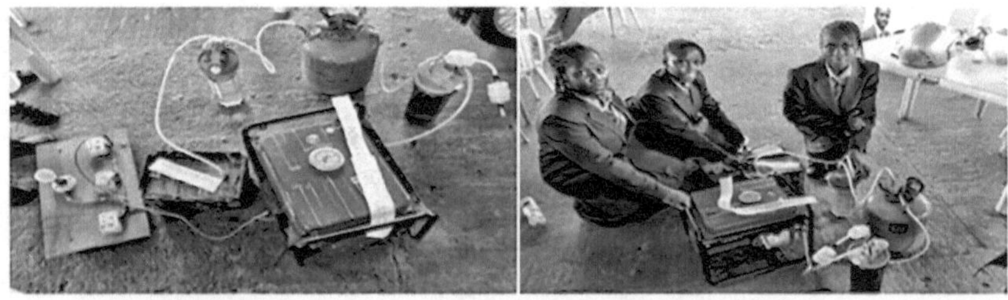

Four female teenage girls between the ages of 14 and 15, the black diamonds from Nigeria, on the continent of Africa, have created a power generator that can be operated with just 1 liter of urine, thereby keeping the 100-W bulb glowing for up to six hours. Names of students who invented a generator that runs in urine;

Duro-Aina Adipola (14), Agindale Apiola (14), Falek Oluadoin (14) and Bello Eniola (15) with the help of their chemistry teacher, injected urine into an electrolytic cell and developed a hydrogen-separating system. In this chapter, we will see in great detail the explanations about it. What friends are you ready for?

Purpose of the Innovation:

While the world is looking for clean energy to reduce the rate of global warming, high school students from Nigeria, with the help of their chemistry teacher, have developed an electricity generating system that can run with urine.

"The main motivation for this project is that deaths due to carbon monoxide released from generators powered by fossil fuel are increasing day by day," the young scientists say. In order to reduce that, Nigerian Energy Grid (NEG) is trying in many ways to develop a generator that does not release carbon monoxide," says the four young scientists, together with the help of a chemistry teacher, to prove that the urine collected can be used to convert electricity. This is the crux of this Innovation.

Urine Generator:

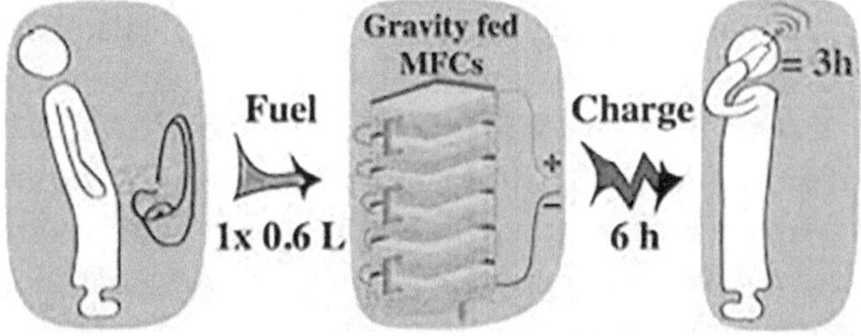

urine into an electrolytic cell and created a system that separates hydrogen. The separated hydrogen, then goes to the water filter for purification and goes into the gas cylinder. The gas cylinder pushes the hydrogen into the cylinder of liquid boraxin, which is used to remove moisture from the hydrogen gas. This purified hydrogen gas is pushed into the generator to produce electricity. Electricity is produced through which a bulb of 100 watts capacity is made to glow for nearly six hours with one liter of urine.

One of these young inventors, Duro-Aina, has proved the Innovation at home by electrifying the lights using urine collected at home. Watch the YouTube video for yourselves. In recognition of the Innovation of these young scientists, the Nigerian government, connects all the public toilets and pay & use toilets/ latrines in a city and produces 450 units of electricity a day with the help of the urine it collects.

In general, if you want to have a paid toilet, you have to pay 5 or 10 rupees. But in that town, go to the toilet and if you urinate, you will be rewarded with two rupees. How can it be great if this happens in our city or town too?

Those to be admired:

We must appreciate this Innovation because in an economically vulnerable country, a people struggling for food, good water and medicine, students struggling for quality education, let their lives shine by turning even the wasted urine into a creative force, producing electricity and flashing a bulb. Let us all will stand up and give a cheerful applause and greet the four young scientists and the teacher who supported them.

What friends! How was our eighth mind-blowing Innovation. I hope you are enjoy reading this book and you will also like this Innovation, which is an example of how success can be achieved if you try, even if it is an IMPOSSIBLE one. Yes. IMPOSSIBLE word itself says I-M-POSSIBLE. "What? Are you going to the bathroom? If you wait a little, you will be given with money in our place as well. Are you ready for?" Well, let's see what the next mind-blowing Innovation.

LIFE-SAVING FAN ROD

"Ultimately, progress and innovation win." - Travis Kalanick

The ninth mind-blowing Innovation:

Another mind-blowing Innovation that we're going to see as the ninth out of ten is the miracle of another student of mine, the "life-saving fan rod". I have already emphasized that my motto is to create YOUNG SCIENTISTS – rather than becoming just a successful Scientist. In that way, "Ram" (name changed for some reason) is another student of mine who was inspired by me, attracted by me, sown the seed of science, performed an achievement as an innovation, created a life-saving noble instrument as an innovation, and won India's "Young Scientist" award. He was a student of a government school in Edappadi village in Salem district. In this chapter, I will explain in detail some of the incidents that took place in his life, the background to the Innovation, and about the Innovation.

Introduction to the Innovator:

Once, I was invited as a Chief Guest to the National Children's Science Congress by National Science Forum (NSF) organized by a rural school where Ram was studying. I would have addressed the audience for almost 5 hours. "What? Five hours?". Yes. I understand what you are asking, "What did you speak for 5 hours?" It's always been like that. The title was: "Thinking of Becoming a Scientist – Ways & Means". After the speech was over, there was a crowd of students around me as such I am like a hero. Many students came and asked, "Sir, can I get your autograph?" I said, "I haven't achieved anything yet. When I succeed, my signature will be autograph for you. You come and get my autograph." Another group of boys and girls said, "Sir, can we take a photo/ selfie with you?" I said "Yes".

Thus, my time keeps passing. The time for my train journey is also approaching. The car that would take me to Salem railway station was also ready. I got into the car and sat down, waved my hand at the students like a politician and left. Suddenly a student came. "Sir, please congratulate me. I have decided that I too should become a scientist like you. This is my dream. Will you guide me?" asked a seventh-grade student.

There was no confusion; he speaks very clearly; he speaks politely. Immediately, a teacher came and interrupted the students including Ram and said, "Students, Sir is running out of time. If he keeps talking like this, he won't be able to catch the train. Let's talk next time," she said with a bit of urgency. I saw a look on his face. He looked at me as if he had lost something. I told him to stop the car for a minute and then got out of the car.

Is it enough just to sow?

"What is this? That's why I'm here. Is it enough just to talk for hours? Is it enough just to sow the seeds of science? Wow. Of the many seeds That I have sown, one has just sprouted as soon as I sow it. Shall I let go of this?" I thought to myself, "All right. May your dream of being a scientist come true. From today onward you are my scientific heir. What is your name?" I asked, and the student replied, "Sir, my name is Ram." Well yes. That's the day and time, when I saw my young, little scientist - RAM. I was confident that he would achieve great things in the future. I hugged him and took a selfie and said, "Okay. Shall I leave?" the young scientist jumped up and said "Bye Sir". I thought it was this that the crop that was grown was visible in the bud.

I couldn't sleep at all on the train journey at night. Was it the impact of the train sound or ram's meeting, or his memories or the dreams he had? The wheel of time ran wildly.

To meet Ramu again:

Two years later, I was called back to the same school as a Chief Guest. This year, to inaugurate the Science Exhibition and to deliver a motivational speech. As soon as I went to school, I was disappointed to expect my Ram to come running and come to see me. My eyes are searching for Ramu. But he was nowhere to be seen. The eyes wave here and there. It's disappointing. I inaugurated the Science Exhibition and keep looking at each project. But the mind isn't there, like a lover looking for a girl-friend.

The tea break is over. Next, I walked into the hall where I supposed to address. Then in the first row was my Ram. He was studying in 9 standard. I realized that my Ram was somehow, head-shaved, very quiet, in a state of despair. I didn't want to go to him and talk to him myself. I don't know the reason.

It will be a half hour since my speech starts. Students have always been addicted to my humorous speeches and songs. They will faint like that. Normally, I will make them to laugh first and then make them to think. Everyone is laughing. It wasn't just my Ramu who laughed at all. Not even smiling. He doesn't even think.

Ramu's sad story:

A question within me was, "Why is this guy like this? It was his dream to become a scientist! It's all Just like that," I kept thinking, and despite myself, I asked him, "What's the problem, Ram? What is your problem? What's wrong with you? What happened to you? Why are you like this? "I just keep asking. A student who was by his side got up and said, "Sir, it's only been a week since Ramu's mother died. For a week now, he hasn't come to school. He's here today because you're coming." The student's answer was shocked at me.

I also approached Ramu, took him close to me, patted him, and before I could ask, "What's the problem with your mother?"

he started crying and crying, not allowing me to speak any more. Then he started weeping and said, "My parents had a fight last week. My father started beating my mother in anger. In that rage, my mother went into the room, shut the door, hanged herself in the fan and died," he cried again.

You are not born to cry. Born to rule. Born to Succeed.

This country would have lost a young scientist if it had consoled him like a common man at that time. Instead, a Guru who makes a disciple, "Ram. You are not just born to cry. You are born to rule. You are born to achieve. No mother should ever hang like your mother to death. Forget about your loss. But, can you find something as a solution for that?" I said, as if in a movie.

He, too, suppressed his cries, looked up a little, looked at me with a straight look and said, "Okay, sir, of course I'll try." I also continued my speech. He also pretended to be excited. The program was completed. Once again, when I thought I could comfort him, when he overtook me and said, "Sir, of course, I'll find something for this," I see a gleam in his eyes. I saw within him a high level of self-confidence. "Whatever help you need, please contact me," I said and left for Chennai.

Six months Later. The thing I thought to myself in my mind was, "This is how all the young people, especially the students, are. They speak well, their curiosity overflows at that moment. The very next minute, the day after, the mind flies towards something else. Then how will they all achieve it?" But my Ram is not like that.

Suicide Report:

One day, the Inbox of my e-mail received a report. The title is "Suicide by Hanging", by Ram, Scientist. With almost commitment, "What is suicide? Statistics on how a person commits suicide. 90% of suicides – hanging to death. Why do they choose to hang themselves and commit suicide? When you commit suicide by hanging their self, what really happens? The suicide attempt by hanging is up to 95% successful," the report, with so many dimensions, was very elegantly similar to the thesis of an accomplished scientist. It was very surprising.

I contacted Ramu again and said, "What Ram, the report is super. But when I jokingly asked him how he was going to stop this suicide attempt, he too, very clearly, needed two more months' time. I don't know what he's going to do. "Okay. If you need any other help, ask me." He said, "As soon as my idea is ready, I will contact you sir. "I don't know anything about electronics. You're the one who has to give the idea." I said "yes", too.

Amazing Innovation:

Not two, not three months, but four months rolled by. Once again, a phone call came from my Ram. "Sir, I've found one. This means that those who commit suicide from home will simply use a saree or dhoti or a rope in a very simple way. They also try to commit suicide by using plastic chairs or stools available at home. The height of this stool or chair is only 1 to 1.5 feet. Put a knot around the neck and knock on the chair or stool under the leg. Then they will be strangled, the conch will be broken and they will die." As he explained, I realized at his Innovation will be definitely a victory.

Ram continued his explanation further. "People who attempt suicide are always over the age of ten or twelve. That means their minimum weight will be 15 kg. Instead of the fixed rigid rod between the fan and the hook at the top, we can replace it with a spring rod. If the sensor, called a load-cell, is attached to a fan blade and monitored through a micro-controller and senses more than 15 kg, the controller releases the spring through solenoid. The spring that we have already loaded will go down to a height of about two feet. Then their necks will not be strangled. They can't even commit suicide," he said without taking a breath. I was just amazed.

I didn't give up either. "A person fails in life and attempts suicide. If they fail in that endeavor, don't you feel it is bad, will they not be upset? If any other suicide attempts continue again?" I asked, a little sarcastically, and he had the answer. "Sir, there's an idea for that, too. When the fan spring comes down, we put a chip in the controller and a song on self-confidence will be played, 'If every flower says life is a battleground'. Otherwise, they will call out to the children, 'Mamma... Mother...'' No, Dad... Let's call him 'Father', he said. "And according to statistics, after 2-3 minutes, they have a change in their suicidal mind. Then they will definitely not commit suicide. They'll forget that effort." I was just as surprised.

Is there so much talent in a student studying in 9th standard? Or were his talents hidden? Was it not denied? Where was the key to being a scientist? The death of his mother? Or is it the concern for this society that no one should die like his mother again? Is he confident that he can?

The pinnacle of Innovation is:

Within three months, with my help and with the help of students of an engineering college, the "life-saving fan rod" was ready. Many times, my Ramu tested it and succeeded in it. One day, when I had the opportunity to meet the Collector of Salem, I explained about this life-saving noble tool. Immediately, they called me and Ramu, arranged for a press meet and asked them to explain the procedure. I put me completely in the background, put my young scientist Ramu in front and demonstrated the instrument he had invented. A triumphant smile on his face. Well yes. He was proud of what he has accomplished. I was also proud to be a Scientist, who created another young scientist.

It is still a matter of pride that Ramu's name, Ramu's invention, has come to all TV channels and newspapers. At the press meet, the Collector was instructed to decide to install this innovation in all government college hostels and government hospitals in Salem district. The technology has been transferred from Ramu's name to a Mumbai-based company. Ramu is also granted royalty rights for the same. To this day, the "life-saving fan rod or fan" is also available on Amazon under the name "Life Saving Fan Rod."

What should we do:

It is not enough just to know about this life-saving, noble tool, but you should also buy it in your home and benefit from it. Some people say, "Am I a fool? Aren't you crazy? I am not a coward enough to commit suicide." I just want to say one thing. Not all those who have committed suicide so far are fools. There are not cowards. There are so many doctors, engineers and teachers. How many people would they have advised or counselled. They would have also said that suicide is cowardice. But when a critical situation in life comes up, when you try to commit suicide, if you have a life-saving tool in your home, you can definitely save a lot of lives.

What friends! Was this Innovation very different? Did you enjoy knowing a noble life-saving tool? Does the student who discovered it seem to hold Ram's hand and console him that I am also your mother! Does it seem to say "Congratulations" enthusiastically? Would you agree that behind every Innovation there is an inspiration? Immediately, through the Internet, order it for Amazon or the company at once that life saving classic fan rod. Are you interested in learning about the next, that is, the tenth mind-blowing Innovation? Are you Ready...

❏

10 out of 10

ANTI-SKIDDING TWO-WHEELER

"Innovation comes from the producer – not from the customer." - W. Edwards Deming

The last, but not the least: The tenth mind-blowing Innovation:

Ten out of ten, finally, we reached the tenth one, another mind-blowing Innovation we're going to see is the "Anti-Skidding or Sliding-free two-wheeler". This is also another invention of my student. Lokesh was a 10th standard student of a government school in Chennai. In this chapter, I will explain in detail some of the incidents that took place in his life, the background to the Innovation, and the Innovation.

Lokesh's interest:

Lokesh is a wonderful student. I have been invited as a Chief Guest in his school for the motivational speech. I met Lokesh for the first time during my visit to his school. His headmaster brought Lokesh to me and introduced him to me. His headmaster said, "Sir, he always talking about projects, inventions, robotics, etc. He too held up his hand full of papers and said, "Sir, I have this idea. I have that idea," he went on stacking up. I was listening eagerly, too. The only thing I told him remains in my mind.

That is the saying of Swami Vivekananda. Titled "The Secret of Success" "Take up one Idea. Make that one Idea as your life. Live on that Idea, Dream on it. Let your brain, muscle, nerves and every part of your body live on that Idea. Leave other ideas alone. This is the way to SUCCESS". I preached the same thing to Lokesh, gave him my mobile number and left. Lokesh used to talk to me on the phone whenever he got time. Sometimes we talk for hours. He will ask a lot of doubts and questions. Continued our scientific seed sowing work.

Army soldier who lost his leg:

After three years of time, the tragedy happened. Yes. Lokesh was studying in Class IX. His father, Mr. Adithyan, was serving as a kavilthar in the army. He was working in Kashmir, the border of the Himalayas. That year, he had come to Chennai for a vacation. He spent his holidays happily with his family. He spent his days at the cinema, the park and the beach with his wife, daughter and son.

One day, while Adithyan was travelling towards his village on Chengalpattu bypass road on his two-wheeler, when he was suddenly turning at a road turn, the vehicle skidded and fell on it. The accident occurred due to the presence of sand on the side of the road. He was dragged along the road along with the bike and stuck between the wheels of the tanker truck on the way and was immediately admitted to a hospital near Chengalpattu.

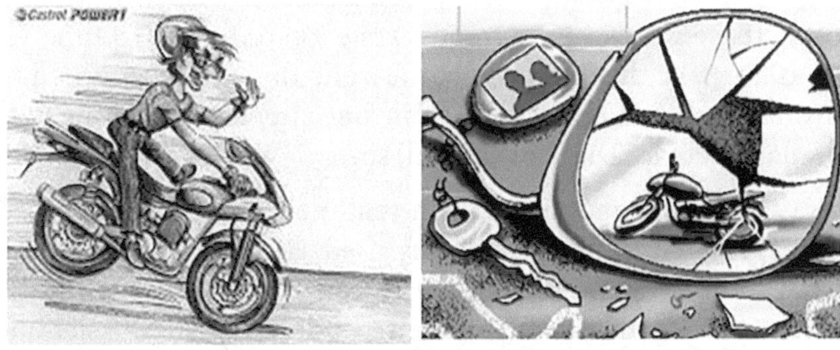

Fortunately, there was no danger to life. But what happened to Adithyan? He was serving in the army on the border guarding duty and was safe-guarding all of us day & night. The right leg below the thigh was completely crushed and severely damaged. So, through the operation, the right leg was completely removed. He was then fitted with a Jaipur prosthetic leg and made to walk half-way. He was also dismissed from service from the army because he lost his leg. After the tragedy, he started and ran a two-wheeler automobile workshop on his own initiative in Chennai itself.

Seed of exploration:

A year passed. So, the family gradually forgot the terrible accident and returned to normal life. No way. His father, Adithyan, used to run the family regularly with the earnings of the workshop. But it was only then that I realized that the impact of this accident was deeply ingrained in Lokesh's mind and in his subconscious mind.

Lokesh asked me the question, "Sir, can I do something for my father, so that he can walk without much problem". I politely replied to Lokesh, "Always find the root cause. Solve there itself. So that It will not happened to others like your father affected."

Again, Lokesh asked "Sir, otherwise Can We find a way for the two-wheeler to go without skidding?". The answer I gave was, "rather than asking 'Can We?', Perhaps say 'I Can', you will get an answer to your question. But if you think or decide, "I can." it's over. These words were a tonic for me too once upon a time. "If we only make this Innovation, the same thing that happened to my father should not happen to anyone else. It will save the lives of many people. That's my dream, sir."

Within three months, Lokesh sent me a report. When I read the report in its entirety, I was surprised. His report was such that I was wondering, whether he is a 10th standard Student or a Chief Scientist. Why does a two-wheeler skid? What is the scientific theory behind it? The statistics of accidents that have taken place so far if the two-wheeler skid, the figures of accidents so far, the flat road, the sand road, the water or mud and the oil spilled on the road. Everything was mentioned in the report: Does the cart skid when it goes down to the angle?

Thereport also contained the information on how it could be prevented. Lokesh's idea was that a two-wheeler has two wheels, doesn't it? Do you understand. When a person drives a two-wheeler, turns to one side, and the angle between the road and the vehicle falls below 13-15 degrees, the vehicle is sure to skid.

At that time, the third wheel, that too on the side of which the vehicle is tilting, automatically ejects on the side of the vehicle. It will come out and start running like a three-wheeler. At that time the two-wheeler won't skid. It is similar to the wheel system that comes out automatically when an aircraft takeoff or lands on the runway.

I was very excited. Happy to find a young scientist again. I immediately called Lokesh and his father Adithyan and congratulated them. "Excellent Lokesh. The idea is superb. And how are you going to implement this?" Lokesh replied, "My father is also a two-wheeler mechanic. I am trying with the help of my father." I said "please proceed".

Two-wheeler that does not slip:

Within a period of six months, the first-level prototype for anti-skidding of the two-wheeler was developed. Yes. Lokesh and his father Adithyan's efforts have resulted in the development of anti-skidding two-wheeler. In fact, they have not developed any new two-wheelers entirely. The developed assembly can be fitted and used on any two-wheeler. They have created such an innovative system, the father and the son. Let me explain it work in a simple manner, in a way that is easy to understand for you. Let's see!

First, when the two-wheeler turns at the turn, you have to calculate the angle between the bike and the road. For that, a system similar to the tilt sensor on the mobile phone i.e. a accelerometer sensor should be installed in the middle of the vehicle, i.e., above or below the fuel tank. The sensor calculates the angle and sends it to the electronics board there. Calculated by the microcontroller installed there, if it goes below 13-15-degree, tilted to the left side,

it will bring out the third wheel on the left. Similarly, if you turn to the right side, it will bring out the third wheel on the right. Once it is back to normal, the third wheel will absorb itself. Since this system works in a hydraulic manner, its movement will be much faster. At the same time, it will be accurate.

Lokesh and his father Adithyan prepared the innovation and first fitted it on his two-wheeler and tested its processing. The first attempt is success. Lokesh, a young scientist, ran like a child behind his father's bike, shouting "Success!!! Success!!!". This scene still remains in my eyes.

After testing this innovation several times, with my efforts, Bajaj, Hero Honda. Having gone to companies and explained its use and its operations, Bajaj has now decided to install the invention in its new models, for which an agreement has been signed to pay an innovation reward and royalty to Adityan, a former army soldier who worked for our country and lost his legs.

What friends! How was this Innovation? This too is a life-saving innovation. Super doper innovation. That's also a mind-blowing innovation, Isn't it? I am able to hear your mind voice saying that "I am ready to become a Scientist? Yes. Inspiring Scientist.". If you are ready, then We are also ready to help you to achieve the SUCCESS.

My dear friends! Dignified Students! Gentle Readers! Can we summarize the excerpts of this "Ten out of Ten" book that we have read so far? Come on.

"Want to know about yourself? Tell me about your friends." Those who realize this always choose good friends. In the first chapter, we learned about a special combination of numbers and the characteristics of people. We learned how best friends should be and how bad friendships should be in "Numbers and Friends".

In the second chapter, we began with "Let's Know Something" and learned about discovery, fiction or invention and innovation, and the connections and differences between them.

In the third chapter, we learn about a life saving invention, the power to drive a pacemaker. In the fourth chapter, we also learned about a universal invention, the "Eight Disease Diagnostics Tool". We also learned that it was a very simple invention at a very low cost.

In Chapter 5, we also enjoyed another innovation of mine, the "Self-prescribing Device". In Chapter 6, we learnt about the invention of a noble life-saving tool, the "Vaccine Cooler" and in the Chapter 7, we learnt about the invention of "Motor Vehicle Powered by Water", which has amazed the world.

In the Eighth Chapter, we learnt about "Self-Operated Wheelchairs" specially developed for people suffering from paralysis or rheumatoid arthritis and in the Ninth Chapter we learnt about "Puncture Free Wheels".

In Chapter 10, we learnt about the rare invention of a "Urine Powered Generator", a power generator that can run on just 1 liter of urine and thereby illuminate a 100W bulb for up to six hours.

In Chapter Eleven, we learned about another fascinating invention, the "life-saving fan rod". It would not be an exaggeration to say that in Chapter XII, we got a clearer understanding of the evolution and process of the invention of the "Skid-free Two-Wheeler".

Dignified Readers! Friends! We have now come to the conclusion of the book. Although I am feeling little painful, that in a few minutes we will be separated in the relationship that has connected us through letters, I am confident that we will meet you again through another book.

Reading is the breath of man. Reading a book is not just an art. It's like healing a wound. Buy good books and read them. Succeed in life. The book is a blessing for all of us. If it is not used properly, the boon is of no use. From you until I meet you again on a good topic.

9 788196 721008